T0289556

THE LITTLE FOX OF MAYERVILLE

Éric Mathieu

THE LITTLE FOX
OF MAYERVILLE

Translated from the French by
Peter McCambridge

QC FICTION

Revision: Katherine Hastings
Proofreading: Anna Prawdzik, David Warriner, Elizabeth West
Book design: Folio infographie
Cover & logo: Maison 1608 by Solisco
Fiction editor: Peter McCambridge

All rights reserved. No part of this book may be reproduced or transmitted in any form or by any means, electronic or mechanical, including photocopying, recording, or by any information storage and retrieval system, without permission in writing from the publishers.

Originally published in French by Les Éditions La Mèche in 2018 in Montréal, Canada under the title *Le Goupil* © La Mèche, une division du Groupe d'édition la courte échelle inc., 2018

Translation copyright © Peter McCambridge

ISBN 978-1-77186-196-0 pbk; 978-1-77186-197-7 epub;
978-1-77186-198-4 pdf; 978-1-77186-199-1 mobi/pocket

Legal Deposit, 3rd quarter 2019
Bibliothèque et Archives nationales du Québec
Library and Archives Canada

Published by QC Fiction, an imprint of Baraka Books.

6977, rue Lacroix
Montréal, Québec H4E 2V4
Telephone: 514 808-8504

QC@QCfiction.com
www.QCfiction.com

Author photo by Céline Chapdeleine

Printed and bound in Québec

Trade Distribution & Returns
Canada and the United States
Independent Publishers Group
1-800-888-4741
orders@ipgbook.com

We acknowledge the support from the Société de développement des entreprises culturelles (SODEC) and the Government of Québec tax credit for book publishing administered by SODEC.

For my father

PART I

"We are linked by blood,
and blood is memory without language."

Joyce Carol Oates, *I Lock My Door Upon Myself*

1.

My whole childhood was nothing but dread, drifting,
and disappointment. And yet I wanted to be happy.

2.

Before me, there was silence. Then I came into the world one misty November morning, and speech with me, and in the previously austere, joyless family home, where no one exchanged a word, only I could now be heard, because I chattered away incessantly, even in my sleep. I'd tell all kinds of stories and tales, I'd perform lines from obscure plays—Cyrano de Bergerac's monologue on his nose came to me as naturally as any nursery rhyme—I'd recite poetry, I knew Valéry's 'The Young Fate' by heart, not to mention most of Verlaine's 'Poems Under Saturn,' and, eyes closed, I'd spout forth whole passages from 'Memoirs from Beyond the Grave' and 'The Songs of Maldoror' in a soft yet firm voice, never faltering, with a quick but clear cadence, accompanied by a knowing, measured smile.

France Claudel, my mother, couldn't stand it. Her lower back pressed against the sink, her face grimacing in disgust, she'd wipe her hands on her apron, stick her fingers in her ears, and sigh with discouragement.

It was hardly my fault if nature had decided I'd express myself like an adult right away. The babbling and gurgling innate to other babies were foreign to me: from the very first day, from the very first hour, I grasped language in its entirety, like a loaf of bread that had yet to be sliced or a perfectly ripe fruit. It was as though I wanted nothing to do with being a baby; I needed to zip ahead, to cut corners so as to enter into language as quickly as possible, and I also wanted to shine, to show that I was superior, that my intelligence, my wit, my knowledge went far beyond those of my parents, those insignificant little people of no importance whom, already, I detested.

The second anyone leaned down over my crib by the kitchen window, where my mother would put me each morning, I would let loose a string of complex words that no one knew, I would reel off long and winding phrases whose meaning escaped the lot of them. When people indulged in baby talk with me, I'd reply, "Whatever's gotten into you? Why are you talking like that?" The handful of neighbours, uncles, aunts, and cousins, all the curious folk who weren't too afraid to come see me—rumour had it I was a devil or a demon— would stare at me wide-eyed, then beat a hasty retreat. My mother would stand off to the side, ashamed, dabbing at her tears with a dishcloth. Those visitors who stuck around would nod off in their chairs, lulled by the monotonous sound of my voice as I recited one thousand forgotten poems. My mother would clench her teeth and curse me. When it was time for supper, she'd wake the dozing guests with a clang of her pots and pans. Before they left, they'd say, "Your son sure is a chatterbox!", "What a talker!", or with a whisper, "Is the child normal?" and they'd cross themselves. My mother, cheeks ablaze and not knowing what to reply, would shoo them outside and slam the door. Then, with no encouragement from my mother, I'd launch into a diatribe about the visitors, giving my opinion on each of them, the meanings of the words they'd used, analyzing their every reaction, their mannerisms, and I'd begin holding forth on behaviourism, Skinner, and the philosophy of the mind, then I'd move on to Freud and Jung without so much as a pause, to the anima and animus, the ego and the superego, and all the other scientific concepts that were especially popular in the fifties but that my mother had never heard of.

France Claudel never understood a thing: the words I used were too obscure, the turns of phrase too complicated; some had fallen out of fashion. She had left school at age eleven.

Quickly I began speaking other languages: German, Romanian, even Hebrew, Greek, and Latin. My mother, a not particularly religious woman, would look to the heavens and pray to God, "When's all this nonsense going to stop?"

The poor woman! Others would doubtless have marvelled at my verbal virtuosity, at the sheer range of exotic idioms I had mastered, but not her. Her embarrassment stemmed perhaps from her upbringing. She was of a generation, a time, when children were expected to be

seen and not heard; and, as far as my mother was con-
cerned, I was making every effort to draw attention to
myself, and *that* she couldn't forgive. That, she would
never forgive.

3.

Deep inside her, she harboured a delectable sorrow: her child.

4.

Even before I set eyes on her, that severe, impervious woman, I understood that she had cursed me. I took hours to come out of her belly; it was, for her, pure torture. She had been waiting for one thing and one thing only: for my body to detach itself from hers, to be rid of her round belly, the tired body of a mature woman, those swollen breasts, the monster kicking at her and who, from inside her uterine cavity, seemed already to be speaking, whistling familiar tunes. But I was in no hurry to leave, and she gave birth three weeks overdue.

Surrounded by kindly midwives, push, pant, and shout as she might, I refused to budge. It wasn't that I was especially comfortable inside her body, it wasn't that I wanted to stay there any longer, because all told it was rather uncomfortable, especially since my mother drank and smoked her way through pregnancy—it really was another time—no, it was the fear of facing the outside world, a world I no doubt already knew would prove hostile to me. It was only after forceps, ventouses, and other assorted instruments of torture that my head finally appeared, leaving the poor woman howling in pain, her body ravaged and her mood very much the worse for wear.

Exhausted by the long and difficult labour, she remained in bed for a good while and it wasn't until eight days had passed that I was brought to see her.

Madame Claudel gave a little shriek when she saw me for the first time. My hair was red, flattened against my head as though with brilliantine. My skin was wrinkled, like a dried chestnut. My complexion was swarthy, my face drawn, with large protruding ears and a long aquiline nose. I looked like a weasel or a fox. I was quickly nicknamed the little fox. It was a name I didn't much care for, since it seemed to me to be associated with a slew of character traits each more ignominious than the last. Back then I had a rather high opinion of myself and, every time I heard that awful sobriquet, my stomach would turn, my crotchety little soul would revolt, and tiny tears of rage would trickle down my Jerusalem artichoke–coloured cheeks.

Unfortunately, the nickname stuck, no doubt since there was some hesitation over choosing my first name, so much so that the people in the village didn't know what to call me.

I remained nameless for so long that one day when the parish priest stopped by, he remarked to my mother that she should really get a move on ("You never know the minute," he said, crossing himself) and so they opted, with a distinct lack of originality, for Émile, my maternal grandfather's name. But at home I was rarely called by my first name. In fact, I was rarely addressed at all.

5.

No doubt to get the better of me, to nip my difference in the bud, to neutralize my precocious oral prowess, my mother soon decided to take me for an idiot. The way she told it, I was nothing but a performing dog, an eccentric simpleton, a gossip and a parrot who, without really understanding, simply repeated words he'd heard here and there. While it was true I had a gift for imitation (I was a good actor and could transform myself into anything at all; I would copy accents and mannerisms, which never went over well since I was assumed to be poking fun), I was much more than a trained myna bird, and it grieved me to see my precocious talents dismissed. By way of revenge, I would break wind and defecate into my fresh nappy, and my bodily odours would mingle with the smells emanating from the kitchen to create a nauseating stench.

Doubtless influenced by my mother, the neighbours, my parents' friends, and our relatives no longer sought to comprehend my words and took my verbiage, with its impeccable syntax but nebulous meaning, to be nothing more than a sophisticated form of childish prattle. They let me talk. I was now reduced to a chatterbox. Visitors would laugh, "Listen to him go, the kid never stops!", "All that gibberish—I don't understand a word!", "How strange he looks with all those wrinkles!"

They peered at me like a curious animal.

I had become domesticated, and I no longer impressed them.

I spoke nonstop, but I had been reduced to silence.

6.

The talkative fox always gets caught. — Proverb

7.

And so, I decided to conform and to play the role expected of me, since showing off my powers of speech seemed to deprive me of any influence. I ceased my jabbering, I abandoned my role of talkative fox and endeavoured to bawl, babble, nap like a baby, cry for my bottle, and smile the touching, inane smiles of an infant. But I would often relapse.

One day a cousin remarked as he leaned down over my crib, "He's cute enough all the same, and he seems so well behaved. He has his father's eyes and his mother's mouth," to which I replied, "Uh, no, I don't have my mother's mouth at all. You're wrong! I don't know whose mouth I have, but it's certainly not hers. I have a big mouth, with fleshy lips. France Claudel has thin, pursed little lips." And on I went, trying to show that my intelligence and general knowledge were worthy of an upper-class family and that I must have been found on the church steps. "France Claudel is not my mother," I shouted.

8.

One day a pair of hands reached down for me in my crib and I'm quite sure they wanted to strangle me.

9.

While I knew very well what my mother looked like, I was unable to say whether I had the mouth or eyes of the man they called my father, for the simple reason that I never saw him. A master baker, his work kept him away all day and a good part of the night. He would leave for work very early in the morning and wouldn't get home until evening, exhausted. He never leaned down over my crib, and whenever I picked up the sound of his voice, it was always far off and distant, as though he was whispering so that I wouldn't hear.

Soon I no longer heard his mumblings, nor even my mother's rebukes and comments, since she moved my crib upstairs, far from the kitchen. It was cold in the bedroom and I felt very alone, so much so that I began to talk out loud and would recite poems and quotations from the great writers to help me fall asleep.

Often sleep would not come, preoccupied as I was trying to imagine my father's features, the waves of his hair, the shape of his nose, the colour of his eyes, the size of his ears. I'd try to imagine his tastes, his desires, even his political leanings. I would formulate hypotheses about the great enigma that marked my entire child-hood: whoever might my father be?

10.

There's none slyer than the fox, and yet the markets are full of their pelts. — Proverb

11.

"Where's Papa?"

"I have no idea," my mother replied without turning around, her hands in the dirty dishwater.

"Shouldn't he be back by now?"

"Yes, probably. Now stop pestering me!"

She tapped her foot as she spoke.

Summer 1953. I was eight years old.

I was small for my age, my legs too short for my upper body, my red hair standing on end, and even though the skin on my face was still kind of wrinkly and a foul yellow pus would occasionally erupt from the blisters that covered my body, I no longer resembled, as I had in my infancy, a dried-out chestnut, thanks in large part to my weekly mud baths deep in the woods as well as to the application of various creams that I would find on my mother's dressing table.

Although I didn't spend much time with him, I now knew what my father looked like. He ignored me, but I would follow him around nevertheless. I would call out to him, "Hey! Show yourself! Show your face!" He would turn around and give me a weary look. He didn't look like me at all.

My father was a solitary man. He would spend his days either by his oven at the bakery or in his van, on his way to sell his bread and cakes in the other villages. He knew everyone, and everyone knew him, but he wasn't much of a talker. People said he was shy and reserved; I found him arrogant, cold, distant.

Like a child on a long journey who asks, "Are we there yet?" every five minutes, I was always asking, "Where's Papa?" mostly, it must be said, to irritate my mother, who would sigh theatrically, at the end of her tether. At times like that, she'd have a face like a bull-dog: short and pug-nosed, with bright round eyes. If she hadn't been so mean, it would have been comical.

"What's for lunch?" I asked suddenly.

My mother turned to face me with her soapy hands. "You'll see soon enough. Who do you think you are?"

The way she saw it, I went about everything the wrong way. I couldn't do anything right. I only ever heard her rebuke me. "Everything you say is incomprehensible... No one understands a thing you say... Stop mumbling... Take your fingers out of your mouth... Don't touch that... Take your elbows off the table... Stand up straight... Stop dragging your feet... Don't scratch your head like that... Stop sniffling... Blow your nose... Stop picking your nose... Go wash your hands... Make your bed... Knife to the right, fork to the left... Don't cross your cutlery on your plate... You don't drink water when you're eating soup..."

My mother took her hands out of the dirty water and wiped them on a gingham dishrag. She looked me up and down, as though seeing me for the first time that day.

"What's with all the bruises on your thighs again? And the scars on your knees?"

"I fell doing a cartwheel."

"You're so clumsy. Forever tripping over your own two feet. Look," she said, raising a hand, "you even have scabs on your face. You're like a damaged piece of fruit."

She stopped talking and looked at her feet.

I stared hard at her. She seemed to be lost in thought and had clearly forgotten I was there.

"Maman."

She sighed.

"What now?"

"I heard there's a carnival coming to Neufchâteau next week. Can we all go together, with Michel, Chantal, and Papa?"

Michel was my brother. He was fourteen years older than me, clumsy as could be, stout, bordering on obese. He still lived with us. Chantal was my sister: blonde, pretty, coruscant. She was seven years my senior.

My mother came closer, dishcloth in hand. She had a menacing look about her, a nasty grimace on her face. How ugly she was. She was wearing her strict-looking glasses, a headscarf. Very 1940s. That was clearly her favourite decade; one look at her wardrobe could tell you that. No doubt she'd once been more fashionable, but now France Claudel had fallen behind the times, and age—she was forty-nine—wasn't on her side: she had no shortage of wrinkles, rosacea, and tiny purplish pimples that her foundation and powder didn't manage to cover up.

"Carnivals," she said between pursed lips, "carnivals are for well-behaved children. You're nothing but a little—"

I interrupted her.

"But Maman, all the other children are going and they're not always good."

"Do you think I have the money for a carnival? Go on, scram," she said, lunging at me. "You're bothering me. Can't you see I'm busy?"

She flicked her dishrag against my bare legs. Then, her eyes mad with rage, she dropped the dishcloth and walloped me on the head. The blood rose to my temples and tears of pain streamed down my cheeks. Then she picked up the cloth, turned around, returned to the sink, and went on washing the greasy plates as though nothing had happened.

I staggered back like a wounded animal and took refuge in the hearth.

Crouched down behind the stove, I kept an eye on her.

Five minutes later, no doubt thinking I'd gone outside, she began to hum a tune that had been popular before the war, glancing all the while through the small, round window out into the courtyard, as though expecting someone.

"France?"

She jumped with surprise.

Louis Ducal, the neighbour who lived across the road, was at the kitchen door. My mother spun around, her hand to her chest. Ducal was dressed like it was winter (it was July): a heavy astrakhan coat that fell to his ankles and a long, red scarf around his neck. His hand was resting on the gold knob of a very elegant cane, and he carried a lambskin notebook under his arm.

"May I come in?"

"Yes, of course," she stammered. She took a step forward, as if to go to him.

He came in, produced a silver lighter from his pocket, and lit a cigarette. He drew on it and, a smile playing at his lips, blew out the smoke as he set down his leather notebook and silver lighter on the kitchen table.

I edged back a little further into the hearth so as not to be seen. I stared at Louis Ducal, the man all the children were afraid of. He was very tall, slim, always dressed in black. He had a slight stoop, his ears stuck out, his face was emaciated and pale, a protuberant Adam's apple rose and fell as he spoke, his eyes were different colours (the left one, a steely blue; the right, sea green), and the whites were infused with blood, a long nose with wide nostrils, two broad black holes from which there escaped the odd curly hair, his skin was dry, and dandruff lay like dozens of tiny snowflakes on the shoulders of his coat and on his red scarf. The children in the village called him the Corpse or the Mummy. From time to time, his pupils would turn red and would instantly hypnotize any child who dared look him in the eye. Ducal lived alone. His wife had died several years previously. They'd found her body at the bottom of a well behind the house. They said she'd drowned herself, and when they pulled her out of the water, her face was half decomposed and had been gnawed at by the rats.

Ducal had a very poor reputation. He was considered violent, dangerous even. One day when Ducal beat a child with a stick because he'd dared trespass on his property, the mayor told him, "You are, Monsieur Ducal, something of a sadist." To which he replied, "No, Mr. Mayor. A sadist derives pleasure from inflicting pain. I derive no pleasure from it, quite the contrary. I am simply compelled to by force of circumstance, because people are animals and because no one who has a modicum of intelligence can tolerate vulgarity or mediocrity. First and foremost, one must ensure that order and discipline be respected, particularly when others have decided to look the other way."

Despite getting on in years—he was rumoured to be ninety—Louis Ducal could at times, much like a man in the prime of his youth and vitality, be spectacularly quick on his feet, and the lines on his face would occasionally disappear, smoothing themselves out as if by magic, making him look twenty, thirty, or forty years younger.

Still crouched behind the stove, I could feel my feet starting to go numb. I saw my mother run a hand through her hair, then tug at her skirt. It was a little short and stopped just above the knee, revealing her petticoat. When Ducal went over to her, my mother dropped the cutlery she was holding and, as she bent over to pick it up, a lock of hair escaped from her bun. My mother straightened up. Ducal drew closer. He raised a fist as though preparing to strike her, but instead, with a movement more nervous and irritated than tender, tucked behind her ear the stray lock that had escaped from the mass of hair. Ducal leaned in as if he was about to kiss her. My mother stepped back, embarrassed. It was at that moment, no longer able to feel my legs, which were by now completely asleep, that I straightened up and collided with the pots and pans that hung over the stove. A frightful din ensued, and my mother and Ducal looked over as one, like a two-headed beast staring daggers at me.

"So you're still here, are you?" she spat. "Always hiding, spying on everyone."

Her hands fluttered in front of her as though she were about to set upon me.

"Get out of here, you filthy beast!" she screamed.

"Filthy beast." She would call me every name bar my own. I don't believe she once uttered my name in her life; and yet Émile is a nice, straightforward name. Two simple syllables, no clusters of complicated consonants, no complex vowels.

My face was scarlet. Ducal stood between me and the door, ruling out any chance of escape.

"This ruffian still giving you a hard time?" he asked my mother, as though I wasn't there. "Boarding school's what he needs."

He cracked his knuckles and moved toward me with a grim, menacing look. He eyed me up and down, apparently disgusted by what he saw, and slapped me hard enough to leave a mark that was still there three days later.

"What a little devil you are!" he proclaimed theatrically, like an actor in a movie from the 1930s.

I made for the door. On my way past the kitchen table, I discreetly pocketed the silver lighter that Ducal had left on the Formica and raced out through the courtyard and into the garden.

12.

The back garden was on a slope, and I arrived out of breath at the top. I began scraping at the ground at the foot of an oak tree, where a little cross was supposed to mark the grave of our old cat Marcus but, in actual fact, it was to help me find where I'd buried my personal treasures: a tin box—an old box that once contained biscuits that I dearly loved but barely had a chance to taste, since I'd be punished every time my mother served them—that contained my most precious marbles, a game of jacks, a pearl necklace, a chain bracelet, a watch, an engagement ring, a signet ring, a toy soldier, a pair of earrings, cufflinks, a gold chain, a minuscule holy medal, a New Testament I'd found on the church steps, a Montblanc pen that had been forgotten on the living-room table and that I think once belonged to Ducal, a screwdriver, an old photo of my father, and a set of keys. I couldn't keep all those things in my room: my mother, who was always poking around, would have found them in next to no time. Her eyes were all-seeing, and nothing in the house escaped her gaze.

I kneeled and pulled the lighter I'd stolen from Ducal out of my pocket. It was a fuel lighter, its owner's initials,

LD, inscribed on it in Gothic lettering. I put it in with the rest of my stash and quickly buried the tin box deep in the ground. I stood up, scuffed the dirt back in place with my feet, and ran backward down the hill.

Ever since I'd read "Prince Paulo the Tyrant," an adventure story featuring Mandrake the Magician in the *Robinson* comics I was so fond of, doing things the wrong way round had become an obsession of mine. The *Robinson* series belonged to my brother, Michel. I found it in his room one day. It was chock-a-block with wonderful stories: "The Circus People," "Chamber into the X Dimension," "The Treasure Hunt," "The Lunar Trip," "Mandrake and Lothar at the Carnival," "The Haunted Range," "The Clairvoyant." Sporting a pencil moustache, black cape, and top hat, Mandrake was an elegantly mysterious magician. He was enigmatically sensuous, borderline pernicious. He had the power to hypnotize the criminals he hunted down, to be in two places at once, to fool his enemies with illusions, and his sophistication and derring-do filled me with an unusual sense of joy that was almost voluptuous.

In my favourite story, "Prince Paulo the Tyrant," Mandrake meets Prince Paulo, who likes to do everything the wrong way round. His Highness insists that his castle must have a roof on the ground and a cellar that looks up to the sky. Since the prince hates the colour green, he decides that in his garden every leaf on every tree must be painted red, a laborious undertaking that the master's slaves, held prisoner on the estate, are tasked with. The prince rides his horse back to front and forces his subjects to fall in line with his strange ways. His life is nothing but a series of inversions, conversions, and transmutations, and, a little sheepishly, since after all the source of my inspiration was a harebrained scheme dreamed up by the vile Prince Paulo, a man capable of great wickedness, I came to realize that anything could be done the wrong way round. Turning things on their head became a way of life, an obsession of mine. I learned to walk on my hands, I walked around the village backward, I went head first down ladders, I inverted words and syllables, I started eating and writing with the wrong hand, I put my pyjamas on backward and slept with my feet on the pillow.

Switching things around led me, naturally enough, given my life as a solitary child, to contortion. No doubt inspired by the perversions of Prince Paulo, who would lock up his prisoners in aquariums and birdcages, I began inching my way in everywhere, into the house's nooks and crannies, into trunks where I would fold myself up, tucking my arms and legs in beneath me until I was as small as possible. I ventured into tighter and tighter spaces and stayed curled up for as long as I could. Often I would no longer be able to breathe or feel my limbs. Violent headaches would strike, and it wasn't uncommon for me to faint.

Pleased with the addition of Ducal's lighter, a fine piece, to my haul, I was making my way backward down the garden that morning when the gardener, Gérard

Thiebaut, whom I hadn't seen trimming the privets, grabbed me by the collar and stopped me in my tracks.

"Where are you going, you rascal?" he asked. "What's all this nonsense? Why are you walking backward?"

He had brown streaks across his face, a bulbous nose crisscrossed with ruptured blood vessels, and a cold sore at the corner of his mouth; on his head, a yellowed handkerchief and, on top of that, a sweat-stained cap.

"To better see behind me," I said.

"Try looking where you're going instead, you idiot! You didn't even see me. You were about to impale yourself on my tools. Good thing I was here to spare you a stay in the hospital, not to mention a good hiding from your mother—and your father!"

He began shaking me like a plum tree at harvest time. I hated the man. He practically lived with us, occupying an outbuilding at the far end of the yard that my parents rented out by the year. The gardener was all over our estate, always spying on me, sticking his nose into every else's business, making notes on his little Rhodia pads about everyone and everything. He could often be seen with my mother who, decked out in a long, no-longer-white linen dress and a frayed straw hat, would help him with the gardening. They would do the weeding, trim the roses, plant blueberries. Then Gérard Thiebaut and she would disappear off together around four o'clock in the afternoon and reappear around an hour later, their hair dishevelled. Gérard Thiebaut would then head down to the village and have a drink at the counter in the grocery store/bar/tobacconist's while my mother made dinner and waited for my father to come home from the bakery.

The gardener continued to shake me like lettuce in a dish towel. I protested and tried to shout over him.

"Let go of me. I haven't done anything wrong!"

"You little scoundrel!"

"Damn you to hell!" I screamed in his face as I managed to free myself.

I ran as fast as I could to the courtyard and went into the house through the barn. I was just about to go into the kitchen and let my mother know that I was heading down to the village to see my friend Max—alias Maxime Bartroz, my best buddy, the friend I'd spend summers with since he was from Paris and only spent his vacations in Mayerville—when, through the half-open door, I spied Ducal, still in the kitchen and kneeling beneath the window in front of my mother, whispering as he clasped his hands together, as though in prayer. My mother and Ducal were speaking softly. You could scarcely hear them.

"No, not now... Stop... You're hurting me... France, what's your secret? ... Don't look at me like that... You promised me... After all I've done for you... That's going a bit far... I'll remember this..."

My mother was sniffling. She was crying. She took out her handkerchief from her sleeve and blew her nose.

Ducal stood up and sighed. "You're so ugly when you snivel," he said, and then asked my mother for a match, grumbling that his lighter had disappeared. Ducal lit a cigarette. She asked him for one right away. My mother, who had picked up the habit during the war, still had the odd cigarette, but behind my father's back since he didn't approve of her smoking. She would go out into the courtyard or stand beneath the arbour in the garden, but never smoked inside.

I stepped back from the door without making a sound, and walked backward and out through the barn. As I crossed the patio beneath the kitchen window, I saw Ducal's silhouette, in profile. He was leaning over my mother, who was clutching the windowsill as though she might faint. He looked like he was about to kiss her. My mother stepped back, but then threw her arms around Ducal's waist, or rather his hips, since she was much shorter than he was.

Ducal, his head deformed by the wavy, bubbled glass windowpanes, resembled an ungainly monster.

13.

At the edge of the woods along the backroad, or even on the village streets, a red fox could often be seen wandering around nonchalantly, with a slight limp and not a care in the world.

14.

Our village was called Mayerville. It was a municipality of two hundred and ninety-five souls, surrounded by farms, arable land, hills, and fields of wheat, barley, and rapeseed; orchards full of apple, damson, and cherry-plum trees; forests of oak and beech that were home to stags and does, wild boar, hares, foxes, partridges, and ravens. Swallows and swifts were a common sight, as well as turtledoves whose cooing grated on my mother's nerves.

The municipality was made up of one main street, commonly known as the Grande Rue. It forked in the middle of the village, where the Petite Rue started and headed west. Both led to a quiet backroad. Our house was on the outskirts of the village, where the road once again split in two: one fork the main road to the next town over, and the other, the Chavée, which ended up a dusty path that led to the Potelon, a wasteland of chalky grass where there'd be the odd soccer game or campfire or even caravans full of gypsies, who the locals would blame for all sorts of problems.

Mayerville was in Lorraine, the land of Charlemagne and Joan of Arc, and it was, at first sight, a village like any other in the region. And yet strange things happened there. Children would sometimes disappear from one day to the next, leaving no trace. They were assumed to have run away, gotten lost, gone to stay with a far-off auntie for a time, but they never came back. Since they were never found, the terrible conclusion was drawn that they had been killed, although no bodies were ever found. Adults would speak of the disappearances in whispers, so as not to alarm the children. They would pledge to keep their children inside, but that simply wasn't feasible in the countryside.

We lived in what had once been the village brewhouse. The business began in 1851 and closed in the 1930s. "We're just like General de Gaulle," my parents would laugh. "We moved into the old village brewery, too!" Louis Ducal, who lived across the road, was said to have been the previous owner, and rumour had it that he sold it to my parents, for reasons that remained obscure, for a pittance.

There were many rooms upstairs. At the top of the stairs, to the left: my bedroom, which we called the red room, a simple room with a few pieces of furniture along a single wall—a queen bed, a toilet with an earthenware washbasin, a ewer, a clotheshorse, a battered armchair, and a small ink-stained desk above which a shelf held a children's Bible, *Poil de carotte*, *The Wonderful Wizard of Oz*, *Jean qui grogne et Jean qui rit*, *The Jungle Book*, and *Alice's Adventures in Wonderland*. The sole window overlooked the main street.

On the other side of the landing: my brother's room, the blue room, which had to be passed through on the way to my parents' room—with its peeling daffodil-yellow wallpaper—and my sister's, with its flaking green paint. When my mother and father went to bed, we could no longer hear them; it was as though they were dead. The same for Chantal. But my brother didn't appear to be much of a sleeper: there was always a shaft of light under his door.

Behind the house was a whole slew of outbuildings. Garden sheds where all kinds of tools were stored; an arbour, with old deck chairs from the thirties that smelled of dust; cellars where beer was once stored in barrels; boxwood hedges; a rose garden; a vegetable patch that ran all the way up to the Mayerville woods. You would get to the garden by walking through the inner courtyard, past a well whose bottom you couldn't see.

The façade—all in white, brown shutters with diamond-shaped holes, repainted every two years—was one of the most elegant in the village. Along the house, from the kitchen to the living room, there was a stone patio where we'd sit in summer for an aperitif, below which there was a cellar where I'd never been. The cellar entrance, which people would automatically step back from on their way past, was a troubling black hole at the foot of a few cracked steps. At night, I often dreamed of that dark hole and would sometimes imagine myself trapped inside, imprisoned by a hideous creature that lived there in the darkness.

15.

I left my mother in the kitchen with Ducal and went down into the village. I walked backward, following the stream. I walked past houses with tired façades, foul-smelling farms, bleak countryside; cowpats every-where, stray dogs, lost hens, sweaty farmers in their overalls. I stopped outside the bakery, hoping my father would see me through the window and wave, but if he did notice me—he was working behind the counter—he didn't acknowledge my presence.

"It doesn't matter," I said out loud as I went on my way. "Just die then!" And I suddenly thought of the rumours that had been circulating in the village for a long time, but that had only recently reached my ears: that my father wasn't my father. The other children called me a bastard and repeated things no doubt picked up from their parents: that my mother was a whore and that none of her children had the same father. The idea that I wasn't my father's son was, it must be said, not so far-fetched. It would have explained a great deal. Monsieur Claudel never spoke to me, ignored me, sighed whenever I spoke to him. He rejected me simply because I wasn't his son. He let me stay in his house, but wanted nothing to do with me. To keep up appearances, I pretended to be outraged by such rumours. I had proof that my father was indeed my father, I objected, hoping that would stop the tongues wagging, but it never did.

I asked my friend Max. Did he know something? What did his parents say? What did the village gossips know? Max was aware of the rumours, he admitted, but he knew no more than I did. He did promise me, though, that one day we'd get to the bottom of it. "It'll be an adventure," he said. "Like a proper police investigation."

I walked past the service station, a simple building with a single pump, where the owner, Monsieur Jacquard, lived with his daughter. Berthe—that was her name—was standing in the doorway. She gave me a big smile and a little wave, but I ignored her. She had thick lips and a huge forehead; she was incredibly ugly. She had the intellect of a five-year-old and everyone made fun of her. Only the tritest of remarks came out of her mouth. Statements no one could disagree with since, although we learned nothing from them, they had the virtue of being true. "When it's hot out, it sure is hot." "Life is life." "A promise is a promise." She liked being around children and would often come talk to us, but we always made it clear that she wasn't welcome.

As I crossed the church square, I saw my brother. He was walking quickly, his head down, and was holding a canvas bag, from which there poked out, not without comic effect, the head of a goose. Michel had been apprenticing with my father at the bakery for a number of years, but since he had a flour allergy, he was soon going to have to stop. I didn't much like my brother, and he hated me. He'd go straight to my mother every time he heard I'd been misbehaving. And he'd hit me any chance he got. One day he walked in on me in the barn. I'd folded myself up inside a crate, practicing my gift for acrobatics in ever-tighter spaces. He yanked me up by the hair and punched me in the face with his podgy fists.

He was a solitary soul and didn't appear to have any friends; it wasn't uncommon to see him wandering through the woods, his jaw clenched, his eyes menacing. Like all solitary men, he was cruel and, like a slain viscount, a Saint Julian the Hospitaller, or a duke of Fréneuse, he went about killing all kinds of defenceless little animals. He would make them suffer before he slaughtered them, that much I knew. I'd seen him in the woods, torturing a pup he'd carried there in a canvas bag. The poor thing was bleeding and no doubt didn't survive the attack by that barbaric individual, his brutality equalled only by his lack of intelligence.

I almost called out to ask him where he was taking the goose—I was sure he was off to slit its throat—but he disappeared down a side street before I could.

As I continued on my way, I passed by the house where Rachel Blanchard, a friend of my sister, lived. Chantal was going out with Rachel's brother, Jean-Christophe, a muscular blond fellow with glistening skin and perfect teeth. His sole flaw was that he was missing a finger on his right hand. As a child, he'd crushed his little finger in a vice he'd been playing with one rainy afternoon. The finger had become infected and had to be amputated. My sister was head over heels in love with Jean-Christophe Blanchard; he was all she ever thought about. Since the Blanchard family and my family were on bad terms—something to do with an orchard and the harvest, I'm not sure of the details—my mother would have been furious had she found out that Chantal was seeing the Blanchard boy.

One day I happened upon the two lovers kissing in a field. Jean-Christophe was fondling my sister's breasts and Chantal was moaning, her eyes closed. When he put his hand up her skirt, her eyes opened wide and it was then that she saw me. She let out a cry and set upon me. "Breathe a word of this and I'll rip out your fingernails. D'you hear me?" I broke free but she caught up with me—the little bitch could outrun anyone—and yanked hard on my ears. She even pulled out a clump of hair from the top of my head. It hurt, but I didn't want to give her the satisfaction of shouting out or crying.

Why did I have to be the one to interrupt so many petting sessions, so many stolen kisses? No doubt because I was quick on my feet. I was everywhere at once. But there was nothing supernatural about my gift for ubiquity. I would endlessly roam the village streets and surrounding roads, since I was always in the way at home, and my mother and father were forever shooing me outside. The result was that nothing, absolutely nothing, escaped my attention.

Just as I was passing by the Blanchard house, I saw Rachel Blanchard and my sister coming out of the barn, each with one hand on her belly and the other across her mouth, cackling like two geese in heat. I called out to my sister and told her my mother was looking for her everywhere, that she needed her, something had happened. "You'd better go home at once," I said, trying my best to look and sound distraught. Chantal stared at me, a suspicious look on her face. "Come on, Chantal, don't listen to him," said Rachel, taking her friend by the arm. Chantal hesitated a little, then wagged her finger at me. "You're lying as usual, aren't you?" I opened my mouth, ready to give back as good as I got, but they turned and headed down the main street. They stopped to look back and stick out their tongues. "You're so childish," I muttered to myself. I could have stuck out my tongue, too, but I had a better idea: I turned and pulled down my pants to show my avenging little ass. Chantal and Rachel squealed and ran off like two startled nuns.

16.

When I arrived at the Bartroz house, the door was wide open and I walked on in without knocking. Madame Bartroz, a pale woman, no doubt from anemia that had been left untreated during the war, was sitting at the kitchen table shelling peas into a large earthenware bowl. On the table, which was covered by a waxed cloth that had been lacerated by over-sharpened knives: a carafe of wine, the *L'Humanité* newspaper, and a cherry-plum pie cooling on a rusty rack. I sniffed. Madame Bartroz turned her head.

"Ah! Émile. Come. Sit down. Would you like a slice of pie?"

"Yes, please. Thank you."

She got up to fetch a knife and plate. I was starving, and I loved desserts. Our father never brought anything home from the bakery: no cakes, just dry bread that hadn't sold. And yet he made fantastic pastries, especially cream puffs, éclairs, and chouquettes. My mother would make floating islands and homemade ice cream on special occasions, but the children were never allowed more than one helping, and aside from big family meals, to which we were not always invited, apart from a simple piece of fruit, we never had dessert.

I devoured my slice of pie and asked:

"Where's Maxime?"

"Out," Madame Bartroz replied. "He's in Neufchâteau with his father, brother, and sister. They should be back soon."

Seeing that I couldn't keep my eyes off the exquisite pie, she asked:

"Would you like another slice?"

"Yes, please."

Madame Bartroz went on shelling her peas as she watched me eat. She smiled. I thought she was very beautiful, even though she was wearing a faded flowery housedress and dusty slippers, her big toe poking out of the worn canvas. The Bartroz family came to stay with the grandmother, Solange Lecuyer, every summer. She lived in Mayerville all year long. At the start of their vacation, Madame Bartroz would continue to dress like a Parisian, but soon she wouldn't bother and would spend the whole day in her housedress; she would forego makeup and give her hair no more than a quick once-over with a comb, paying no heed to the straggling locks that gathered on her head.

I heard someone cough in an adjoining room, the bedroom on the street side that was known in Lorraine as the *belle chambre*, or the nice bedroom. It was the grandmother who, weakened by rheumatism and other illnesses I couldn't name, was now bedridden for a good part of the day. No one really knew how the old woman, once her children left for Paris, managed to make it through the winter in a rainy village where it often snowed from December to February, how she kept warm, what she ate. It was as though she went into hibernation: we never saw her and she seemed only to come back to life when the Bartroz family came back in the spring.

Madame Bartroz stood up and went to see to her mother. I took advantage of her absence to help myself to some more pie, just a sliver, not enough for anyone to notice.

Suddenly the sound of a car, doors slamming. Through the kitchen window I could see Monsieur Bartroz and his children—Max, Julien, and little Marie— getting out of the family Panhard.

Max Bartroz was my one and only friend. He appeared in the summer of 1951. At first, I didn't much like him. I thought him haughty and distant. I figured, "He's a Parisian. He won't speak to me." Then one day Max and I crossed paths behind the church and he stopped just in front of me, his face almost pressed against mine.

"Are you the little fox?"

"What?"

"The little fox. That's what they call you, isn't it?"

I didn't reply and kept walking. How I hated that name!

He followed me and called out:

"Do you want to come fishing with me tomorrow?"

I stopped and turned. I didn't really know what to say. I wanted to say no. I thought it was a test, that he wouldn't show up or that he'd make fun of me. I said yes, shyly.

The next morning I got up early and went to meet him where he'd said. Max was there. I saw him when I was still a good distance away and ran toward him. We went to the banks of the Vair and sat beneath a willow to fish. We would later boast of having caught—and released—all kinds of trout, gudgeon, and pike, but in reality, we didn't even get a nibble. We spent the rest of the day playing in the meadows and went home late that afternoon, thoroughly sunburned.

The following morning Max came by my house. First he called, "Come on, little fox!" I was in my room. The window was open. It was only when he shouted, "Émile, let's go, it'll be fun!" that I went over to the window and said, "OK, I'm coming!"

Before I met Max, I didn't know what friendship was. No one in the village would play with me.

I was a wild child, always running through the woods, far from everyone. A solitary being in a hostile world. Someone who spoke without drawing breath, but had no one to talk to. Max changed all that. I hadn't known him for very long and perhaps our friendship wouldn't last, but now I knew what it was to have a friend.

Little Marie was the first to come into the kitchen. She walked right up to me and offered me the plums she was holding. I took them. They were nice and warm and juicy. I popped them in my mouth and their nectar ran down my chin. I turned bright red and Marie, who had big black eyes and skin so white it seemed translucent, with tiny blue veins below the skin, like trickles of water trapped in the ice of a frozen stream, burst out laughing.

Max's father came into the kitchen, his arms weighed down with boxes. He had blue eyes, tanned skin like an Arab, hair that ran in waves across his head; he was a good-looking man. He had served in North Africa, had once been a communist, then by turns a packer, courier, storekeeper, gendarme, and private detective. He gave my red hair a friendly tousle and set the groceries down on the table without a word.

Then in came Max and Julien, laden with bags.

"Ah, Émile! You came!" Max exclaimed.

He handed the bags to his mother.

"Let's go into the yard," he said, dragging me by the arm.

We played ball, then after a while, once we grew tired of that, we decided to walk the paths around the village. Before we went out, Max took the rest of the pie and a box of matches that was on the stove.

In a field, we began burning straw, then we tried to get a bull to chase us, but the animal was too tired and lazy. Later, at the far end of the village, we threw stones at the windows of an old building—to see who could break the most panes—and we were about to head back since it was getting late, when a boy we'd never seen, an intriguing-looking older boy, came over. He had a thick lock of hair that hung over his right eye and his left ear was pierced with a small, shiny ring. With his short-sleeved linen shirt and flannel shorts with multiple pockets and mother-of-pearl buttons, he cut a fine figure, even though he was a little scruffy, with brown streaks across his face and on his knees.

"Got a smoke?" he asked in a husky voice.

I just stared at him, and Max shook his head.

"We don't know you," said Max. "Where are you from?"

"Not from around here."

"You lost?" I asked stupidly.

"No, just wandering around," he replied, smiling. But it was a sardonic smile; there was nothing warm about it.

The sun disappeared behind the mountain to the west. It felt cooler all of a sudden. I wanted to tell Max it was time to go back, that I couldn't be late for supper, that my mother, that tyrant, that old shrew, would be sure to grumble then punish me.

"I have something to show you," the boy said.

"What is it?" asked Max, trying to sound indifferent.

The cold began to cut through me as the temperature continued to drop.

"What if I told you I was carrying a knife? A long, sharp knife?"

I stepped back with a shudder.

"Show us," Max said defiantly.

I was afraid the stranger might attack us with his knife, that he might try to hurt us. I knew how to look after myself, but not against boys much older than me and definitely not against a young man wielding a knife.

He stood there and didn't speak. His eyelids fell, as though he was about to fall asleep standing up.

"What's your name?" Max asked.

"Pim," he said, his eyelids still low.

Then he raised his eyes and said:

"I'm with the carnival in Neufchâteau. We've been there three days."

"Are you going to come to Mayerville?" I asked shyly.

"Probably, but not right away."

"Show us your knife then," said Max with bravado.

Pim pulled a tortoiseshell sheath from his pocket and, from the sheath, a knife. The blade was long, threatening, provocative.

"I really need to go," I said, worried now.

"I'll show you what I can do with it," the boy said, rolling his shoulders back.

He took aim at a tree some ten metres away and sunk the knife straight into the trunk.

Max whistled, impressed.

"Are you a knife thrower with the carnival?"

"No, not at all. Well... not really."

If we had it in us, Pim added, we could stand against a tree, an apple on our head, and he'd take aim and slice the fruit in two with his knife. Max burst out laughing and said, "No, no thank you!"

Max began asking all kinds of questions and Pim replied enthusiastically. He talked about the shows, the animals that travelled with the carnival, the magician, the latest attractions. It was fascinating and I was no longer in a rush to leave, but I was worried because my mother and father always insisted we were sitting down at the table at seven o'clock sharp.

"Come with me," said the boy with the knife. "I found a cave we can hide in. I have all sorts of things there—I'll show you. I can sell you some, if you like. Do you have any money on you?"

"It's getting late," said Max awkwardly.

"It is," I sighed. "I really have to go."

The young man gave us a look as sharp as the tip of his knife and, without a word, motioned with his hand as if to say goodbye or "too bad for you," and walked off down the path.

"What do you make of him?" Max asked, turning to me.

I shrugged.

"I really have to go," I said. "I'm going to get in trouble."

"OK," said Max. "See you tomorrow."

I headed north and Max went south.

I cut through the woods, since it was already late. I ran, stumbling and tripping over roots as I went. I scratched myself on the brambles and grazed my legs in the bracken. Dead branches cracked beneath my feet. People said you had to keep an eye out for old shells from the war, but I'd never seen any and there had never been any explosions so I paid no attention to where I put my feet.

By the time I got home, the whole family was sitting around the table. Mouths were chewing, hands busy with knives and forks, bread, salt, pepper. I went to wash my hands at the sink and sat down, trembling a little as I unfolded my starched napkin. My plate was piled high with food. Just as I picked up my fork, my mother brought her fist down hard on the table and roared:

"Don't bother. You're too late!"

My father jumped. He almost choked, and coughed into his napkin.

"Straight to bed without supper," she said, her eyes angry. "That'll teach you. Where are your manners? Coming home at this hour. And not even an excuse! Not a word. Nothing. Aren't you ashamed of yourself?"

I stood up. My father didn't dare look at me. My sister, though not overly fond of me, seemed to take pity on me. I went straight up to my room, pulled on my pyjamas and, without saying my prayers, slipped beneath the grey sheets, which, curiously, like all our household linen, bore the initials LD, embroidered in red. I jerked the dark red eiderdown over my head and, despite my irritation at my mother's meanness and my rumbling stomach, I fell asleep in no time.

I was awoken an hour later by the sound of footsteps in the loft. The huge loft- once used to dry the brew-house hops—was one of the few places in the house where I never went, because I didn't have the key. I had managed to steal the spare key for every room in the house, except for the loft. I longed to explore up there, because I knew from having spied on my mother many times that that's where she stored documents, letters, and old postcards in wicker trunks and cardboard suitcases, all kinds of treasures that I was convinced—I could feel it—would reveal my father's identity.

Minutes later I head a series of dull thuds, as though someone had fallen or was moving something heavy, and I thought I could even make out a sigh and stifled sobs. I felt a strange, sad pleasure upon hearing them and, lulled by those gentle murmurs, I went back to sleep.

I woke up again around four o'clock, my mouth dry, my body sticky with sweat. I got up and drank all the water—practically without drawing a breath—from the ewer on the little washstand. I opened the window and the shutters to let in a little fresh air and rested my elbows on the window rail. I glanced across the street. Ducal's home, lit up by the moon, stood there, menacing and magnificent in the night. A window to the right caught my eye. I thought I might have glimpsed the outline of a young man. Surprised, I shuffled back into the darkness a little so that I wouldn't be seen. The young man's face approached the window, his forehead touching the glass. It was Pim, the boy with the knife that Max and I had met late that afternoon. What was he doing at that hour in the dilapidated house, its shutters broken, its once-immaculate stucco now yellowed and brown, its garden walls covered in moss?

I wasn't dreaming. Pim was waving from the window, motioning for me to come join him. How could it be? Ducal lived alone. Pim and Ducal didn't know each other.

I closed my eyes for a few seconds and when I opened them again the silhouette had disappeared. I waited for a long while, but Pim didn't come back.

I closed the shutters and the window and curled up in my bed. I had trouble falling back to sleep. I tried to figure out the link between Pim and Ducal, and it wasn't until dawn that I was overcome by sleep. I awoke with a jump around eight o'clock. The sheets beneath me were soaked through and the strong smell of urine, acidic and almost animal in nature, permeated the room.

17.

Since I didn't get up, paralyzed as I was by shame, my mother realized right away that I had wet the bed. She came into my room triumphantly. "It stinks in here," she cried, loud enough for the whole house to hear. She hurled my eiderdown to the floor and yanked on the sheet. My small body in its striped pyjamas lay at the centre of a corona that ran all the way to the edge of the bed. "Isn't that unfortunate," she cried. "At your age!"

She pushed me out of bed, grabbed the sheet, and went over to the window, which she opened along with the shutters. Then she unfurled the proof of my disgrace over the windowsill.

"Wet the bed again, did he, that little good-for-nothing?"

I recognized Ducal's voice.

"Yes," she replied, leaning out the window. "At this rate, he'll be back in nappies soon."

I heard our neighbour guffaw. Then he said:

"I was on my way over to see you, my dear, but I can see you're busy."

"Come in an hour. It'll be quieter then."

Ducal must have made an amusing gesture because my mother laughed.

I was standing in the middle of my bedroom, steeping in my soaked pyjamas. I waited. My mother turned and said:

"Well, go on! Get undressed and go to the kitchen."

She followed behind, prodding me down the stairs. She washed me at the kitchen sink with a rough glove that stung my skin and a nauseating brown soap. I was terrorized by the thought of my father, my brother, my sister, even Ducal, walking in while I stood there naked for all to see.

My mother dried me, grating my skin with an old, rough towel, and told me I was to be punished twice: first for coming home so late and now for having wet the bed. I ran up to my room to get dressed, mumbling that it wasn't fair. When her sheets were soaked in blood, dark clots of it, and some sort of disgusting cherry-red jelly, no doubt the result of a miscarriage or even an abortion, no one ever hung them out the window.

Since I was being punished, I stayed in my room and occupied myself as best I could. I took the game of jacks out of my pocket and practiced flipping them.

Some time around noon, my mother called upstairs to tell me lunch was ready.

At the table, where normally we didn't look up from our plates and where we were forbidden to talk, or even to make a sound with our cutlery or our mouths—woe betide anyone who slurped their soup—I dared to ask:

"Did anyone hear that noise last night?"

"What noise? You're going mad, my boy," said my father. "It was probably a rat. We'll have to change the traps."

"What are you afraid of?" my sister asked. "Think a monster's coming to gobble you up?"

She tickled me all over and I squirmed. I couldn't abide her touching me.

"Stop that!" shouted my mother. "You know very well your father doesn't like you talking at the table, let alone all that wriggling around."

He looked at her in surprise.

"Behave yourselves," she continued. "Where do you think you are?"

My sister pouted while my father served the rabbit in mustard sauce, accompanied by stringy green beans and sticky flageolet beans, that we were served once a week, every Sunday. Aside from the head, every part of the animal was there in the flat earthenware dish, even the rump my mother was so fond of. Much of the conversation between my mother and father revolved around food, more precisely about what we were eating and what we would be eating that evening, the next day, and the rest of the week.

After the meal, I went back upstairs since I was still being punished and wasn't allowed to go out. On the landing, I noticed the door to Michel's room was open so I went in. On his night table, beside a plastic, glow-in-the-dark Virgin Mary that had been a great source of wonder throughout my childhood, I noticed a brown notebook I'd never seen before. I sat down on the bed and began to flip through it. I came across an enigmatic passage, some sort of poem penned by a trembling hand in purple ink: "By the pond, I saw you. So young, so ravishing. Immediately, something stirred inside me. I kissed you. You did not move. Your lips were exquisite. I stifled a cry. I sucked the blood from your mucous. Your blood now runs through mine. O, my beloved, be with me for all eternity. I love you, I love you so much. I'll never let you go."

I pocketed the brown notebook, got up, and tiptoed back out of my brother's bedroom.

18.

It was a fine summer's day and children were playing outside. My window was wide open and I hovered behind the lace curtains. I still wasn't allowed out of my room. Suddenly I heard Max's voice. He called out to my mother, who must have been on the front doorstep.

"What are you doing here?" she asked him.

"Hello, Madame Claudel," Max said reverently. "I've come for Émile."

"What for?"

"To go play. I haven't seen him all day. He's not sick, I hope..."

"He's been punished," she said.

Max asked:

"For how long?"

"Until tomorrow morning. He came home late. I assume he was with you, was he? Tell him he's not to be late. Oh, and Émile wet the bed, too. There you are, you're all up to date now."

I leaned out the window and saw my friend turn, his head lowered, and go back down the main street, dragging his feet in the dust.

19.

You run breathlessly through the starry night as though pursued by a thousand beasts, red hair in the wind, heart pounding.

20.

The next morning, I got up at first light. I was eager to see my friend Max again, to explore the pathways and the woods. I hadn't wet the bed and I was proud of myself. Following the example of *Poil de carotte*, a story I'd read at the start of the year with great interest and enthusiasm, I hadn't drunk anything all day in order to keep my sheets dry that night.

I went into the kitchen and exclaimed:

"Maman! I didn't wet the bed."

She looked me up and down, squinting as though she didn't understand.

"Can't you say good morning first?"

"Good morning, Maman."

I waited for her to comment on my exploit, but it never came. She turned back to her dishes and said:

"Take a piece of fruit for breakfast. There's no bread or milk left."

"Already?"

"What? What did you say? You be careful, boy. I've had enough of your insolence. If you carry on like that, I'll send you to boarding school."

I took a peach from the bowl on the sideboard and kneeled on a chair.

"Sit properly," said my mother.

I did what I was told, but stuck out my tongue as soon as her back was turned. I bit into the juicy fruit, then discovered to my horror that the pit was hollow and teeming with ants. I dropped the peach onto the table and the ants fled; soon they were making their way across the Formica in single file. Since my mother still had her back turned, I soundlessly spat into the bin the monstrous flesh that had almost made me vomit, and chucked the rest of the fruit into the household waste. Darned ants, they were everywhere: in boxes of biscuits, in the sugar jar, in the breadbin. They must have been nesting in the cabinets and under the floorboards. My mother pretended not to see them, but the house was infested.

My mother was going about her household chores and paid me no heed. I went out. Walking down the main street, I passed by the school where Mademoiselle Lavallée, one of the two village schoolmistresses, was sitting by the door on a stone bench, in her summer clothes, a book in hand. She gave me a shy little wave with the tips of her fingers, which I did not return. Mademoiselle Lavallée was in charge of the boys' class and Mademoiselle Fortin, a tall woman with black hair who reminded us all of Maria Casarès, taught the girls. Despite their different surnames, the children were convinced they were sisters since they looked so alike.

Some of the village gossips said they were lesbians. I didn't need to ask what the word "lesbian" meant, since I understood everything, my insight equalled only by my wiliness. Nevertheless, I doubted that our dear schoolmistresses were lesbians, that is, until the day I went back to class to pick up a book I'd forgotten and saw them kissing furtively in the hallway. They had their backs to me and no doubt thought that all the pupils had gone. I had no intention of disturbing them and turned on my heel, trying to make as little noise as possible but, just before I reached the door, in my haste I dropped my satchel. The two young ladies spun around in horror. "Did you see us?" Mademoiselle Lavallée asked. "Yes," I replied boldly. "You won't say a word?" Mademoiselle Lavallée begged. "Promise us," said Mademoiselle Fortin, eyes glistening and lips quivering.

Since I didn't say hello, Mademoiselle Lavallée lowered her head and returned to her summer reading. I went on my way and walked past the church. I decided to go in. I dipped the tip of my right hand in the holy water and made the sign of the cross, only the wrong way round.

To my left stood a statue of a saint that dated back to the sixteenth century, its pedestal bearing an inscription in Gothic characters: *Sancte Lamberte ora pro nobis.* The saint was wearing a long tunic and coat, and was holding an open book. I felt as though he was gazing at me disapprovingly and I stuck out my tongue. I walked down the main aisle toward the altar, on which there lay several bunches of plastic flowers. On the left, there was a second statue, a pietà holding her son's body with one hand, her head turned to the side, wiping away her tears on her dress with her free hand. I kneeled before the Virgin and blessed myself, this time the right way round, since two inversions in a row was to be avoided; it brought bad luck and I had too much respect for the Blessed Virgin, for whom I would never have shown a lack of consideration. I prayed for her to give me a sign: Was there any truth to the rumours? Was Joseph Claudel my father? And if he wasn't, then who was? I begged her to answer all my questions. But she looked at me forlornly, as though she had little time for tittle-tattle.

I was lost in prayer when suddenly I heard a woman whispering. I turned around and saw a shape, a shadow in the nave. There weren't many windows, and it was dark. A handful of words, murmurings, reached my ear: dove, cigarette, hat. They made no sense, but those words that seemed to come out of nowhere chilled me to the bone. It felt as if the temperature had dropped ten degrees in a matter of seconds. I stood up and hurried to the exit.

On my way down the church steps, I saw the parish priest opening the little gate to the cemetery. He was holding a bouquet of carnations. I was about to cut left and leap over the wall to avoid him, but he spotted me.

"Something to tell me, my child?"

"No."

"Do you want to confess?" he asked, drawing closer.

I lowered my eyes and didn't reply.

He looked at me ruefully.

"You missed catechism again," he said suddenly. "I'll have a word with your mother."

"Oh no, not my mother!" I cried, lifting my arms to heaven. "She'll beat me again."

"Beat you? But..."

"Yes, with a big belt or a piece of wood. She's already broken dozens of straps across my back. She doesn't have any left."

"Aren't you exaggerating a little?"

"No. She enjoys beating me black and blue. She's very strict, Father. I'm covered in hematoma."

"Hematoma?"

The priest furrowed his eyebrows. He was handsome. Fair hair, delicate skin, fine fingers, feminine little wrists. He can't have been more than twenty. He took a step forward and put a hand on my shoulder.

"Run along now, child. May God protect you."

I pushed open the cemetery gate and whistled as I walked off.

As I crossed the church square, I bumped into the Gypsy. A yellow Gauloise hanging from his lips, he was sitting by the old fountain, legs spread, bare feet in his shoes, shirt unbuttoned, skin the colour of baked clay, two enormous pectoral muscles, nipples the colour of blueberries. I stopped to look at him and noticed that he had a large hole in the knee of his pants.

"Want my photo?"

"What?"

"I said, you want my photo?"

Robert Bentat, a.k.a. the Gypsy, was my mother's gardener before Gérard Thiebaut. People said that before I was born, he lived in the apartment at the end of our courtyard, but I couldn't see how that was possible since, with no small amount of prejudice, I must confess, I had imagined him living in a caravan instead. One day I asked my mother if she could confirm he had once lived with us, but she just shrugged her shoulders. I knew that she found him very attractive, since I'd overheard her telling a neighbour that he had "a body to die for." The expression had struck me as vulgar coming from the mouth of my mother, a woman who after all was married and about to turn fifty.

"Scram, idiot!" the Gypsy said, staring daggers at me.

I didn't move.

I gazed in admiration at his muscles.

Perhaps *he* was my father.

He made to get up.

"Get out of here, before I have you for breakfast."

I bolted down the main street, not stopping until I was outside Max's house where I finally came to a halt, out of breath, head down, hands on my knees.

21.

The Bartroz home was right by the main road; there was room for no more than a bench between the house and the street. The stream into which wastewater and litter were still dumped flowed right past their front door. A pile of manure, which attracted a cloud of ravenous insects and whose smell was a constant bother to the Bartroz family, separated their home from the farm next door. It was to that farm that Max and I would go, along with the other children from the village, to see the calves being born in the cowshed.

Rectangular and perpendicular to the street, the Bartroz house was a typical Lorraine home. It had once belonged to a farm labourer and comprised four parts: the dwelling, the barn, the stables, and the cowshed. The dwelling had three rooms, one after the other: a bedroom that looked onto the main street, a kitchen, and a back bedroom. The loft had been converted into a dormitory, and that was where the Bartroz family slept.

The door was wide open. I stepped inside and was surprised to find Madame Bartroz, standing with her back pressed against the dresser, swigging wine straight from the bottle. She hadn't seen me come in and I was about to leave when she turned and saw me, her eyes wild and guilty. She removed the neck of the bottle from her mouth, making a funny popping sound, wiped her lips with the back of her hand, and put the bottle back in its place. She looked tired—her face sagged and two dark shadows ringed her eyes—and told me without me having to ask:

"Max is in the yard."

I went outside through the barn to see my friend. Little Marie, holding a pair of knitting needles and cradling a ball of wool in her lap, was in the yard, sitting in a little wicker chair. Max was lying on a blanket, reading a comic book.

"Hi Émile. Want to go fishing?"

"Sure."

Max leapt to his feet and grabbed two of his father's fishing rods that were leaning up against the wall. Before we left, his sister handed me a little strip of wool.

"What's this?" I asked.

"Maman is teaching me to knit. I'm practicing. I just did a row. Here, it's yours," she said with a sad little smile, dropping the wool into the palm of my hand.

I stammered a shy "thank you" and turned beet red. That piece of wool remained nestled in my pocket for months. I'd take it out in winter and rub it against my cheek as I fell asleep, turning my thoughts to the Bartrozes, who were back in Paris. One day my mother found it in my bed and threw it out. I fished it out of the dustbin, washed it at the village fountain, and dried it in the sun. The wool had gone all fluffy. For added safety, I decided it would be more prudent to keep it in my tin box with my other treasures.

"So, shall we go?" Max said suddenly.

"I'm coming."

Max and I fished for about an hour on the banks of the Vair, but the fish weren't biting. We decided to go swimming instead. Once we were in the water, Max made a bet with me: if I jumped from the bridge, if I had it in me, he'd give me a franc's worth of candy. The bridge was fairly high, and there were rocks to the left that would be best avoided. The river was quite deep at that spot. Diving was surely not an option, but what wouldn't I have done for a franc's worth of candy (not twenty centimes', not fifty centimes', but a whole franc's worth!) and, more to the point, what wouldn't I have done to impress my friend Max! I got out of the water, went to stand in the middle of the bridge, and stepped over the guardrail. After a moment's hesitation, I went for it. My dive impressed Max and he was keen to follow my lead; he dove in, too. His dive wasn't as elegant as mine and I told him so, which led to something of a friendly competition. Who could do the best dive? Needless to say, I wanted to do a back dive, too. I didn't manage to pull it off and ended up swallowing several mouthfuls of water. Max had a good laugh.

We were floating on our backs to rest a bit when, at the side of the river, we saw a girl—or was it a boy?—

watching us, a hand up to shield against the sun. He or she was wearing polyester pants, a white short-sleeved shirt, and heavy clogs.

"What are you up to, boys?"

I recognized the voice right away: it was Berthe, the garage owner's daughter. Her tongue was too big for her mouth. She had a lisp.

We didn't reply, and after a few more strokes we got out of the water and continued to horse around. Berthe kept on watching us. Max called over to her and told her she should dive in, too. She shook her head and laughed at the same time. "No, no, no, we're not allowed, we're not allowed," she kept saying. Max walked over to her and whispered in her ear that she shouldn't be scared, then he kissed her on the cheek. She blushed and said, "OK, then," and went off to get undressed behind a tree. She came back wearing her panties and we saw right away that she had taken off her brassiere, too, which made us laugh. "Do you think she'll do it?" I asked Max. "I don't know, I think so," he said. "Go on, dive!" Max shouted. Berthe walked up to the edge and shrieked. "Close your eyes and hold your nose," I told her. She hesitated for a good while. "I bet she belly-flops," Max said, waving to her. Berthe took a step back and pulled a face. "Come on, Berthe. Jump and I'll kiss you on the lips!" said Max, winking at me. Berthe inched forward. She stepped up onto the guardrail, which wasn't very high, and stood up straight, ready to dive. You would often see her grinning inanely, but now she was deadly serious. She pinched her nose, squeezed her eyes shut, and just before she jumped, she shouted, "I can't swim!"

22.

Sometimes, I would catch my mother sitting on the edge of a chair, a rag over her shoulder, looking drained, eyes wet. I wouldn't say anything, but as she rubbed her right hand along her thigh, she'd look me in the eye and say, "My legs won't carry me much longer. I'm tired." I would look at her idiotically, not knowing what to reply.

23.

On the back of an old, yellowed receipt, I drew up a list of the men in the village who might have been my father. Beside each name, I gave them a score from one to ten. Ten points meant they were the man on whom all hopes were pinned, the man who stood the best chance of being my father. One day my mother found the list under my mattress and threw it away.

24.

One morning, instead of taking the main street, I took to the paths behind the houses. I stole fruit from orchards, I peed against walls and in people's vegetable gardens. I saw two little girls watch from a window as I urinated on a row of leeks. Once I'd thoroughly watered the vegetables their parents had so carefully planted, I walked up to the window, pulled down my pants, and waved my pecker around in my right hand, sticking out my tongue at the two little girls, who retreated aghast into the penumbra of the room. I laughed as I skipped away.

I went off to find Max, as usual. I hadn't seen him in four days. He was visiting an aunt in Nièvre with his family.

When I arrived at the Bartroz house, the kitchen was empty. "Max!" I shouted and I heard his voice. "In Grand-mère's room!" he cried. I headed to the back of the kitchen and turned right. I found Max sitting on a chair beside Solange Lecuyer's bed. She was in the middle of telling him a fantastical local tale. A bout of rheumatism had kept the old woman in bed for three days. The bedside table was covered in framed photographs of her children and grandchildren, and on the walls hung antique paintings by local artists: landscapes, craggy peasant faces. A large stoneware vase of rhododendrons in each corner. Max stood up and came over to me. The time had come, he whispered, to find out more about the rumours circulating about my father. Max's grandmother, who had been born in the village and had spent her whole life there, knew everything about the locals. "She'll be able to tell us," Max whispered, his eyes gleaming.

He went to sit down on the bed and motioned for me to take the chair. I went over and sat down. A whiff of sweat, still-damp sheets, undigested garlic. The widow was all hair, duvet above her plump lips, hair sprouting from her armpits, skin as fine as crêpe paper, deep lines on her forehead, little rotten teeth, and breath like a cat after its nap.

"Why, who are you, my child?" she asked. "I don't know you."

Max replied for me.

"This is Émile, Émile Claudel," he said. "You know him, he's my friend. He lives up at the top of the village."

"Oh, my poor dear," she said. "I don't recognize anyone anymore. Isn't that a shame?"

I didn't know what to say to that, so I held my tongue. Only a child can easily skip their turn in a conversation.

"Now, where was I? I'll start again from the beginning."

Max coughed and said, "Grand-mère, since Émile is here, we have a few things to ask you. You know all

82

about the village. I'm sure you'll be able to help." Max gave me a wink.

"There are rumours going around about Émile's father. People say Monsieur Claudel isn't his father."

She hesitated for a moment and then she exclaimed:

"Ah, tittle-tattle! You mustn't believe everything people say."

It seemed to me that she gave Maxime a knowing smile. She turned to me and took my hand.

"I knew your mother well. We took her in for a while during the war. She wasn't well. She had what's known as a fit of hysterics. That was the summer of 1944. She was so lonely. People used to say all kinds of things about France Claudel, especially once her husband was captured, about the G.I., about Louis Ducal, about what she was doing in Neufchâteau."

She stopped suddenly, as though she'd said too much.

Her hand, covered in liver spots and all shrivelled like a dried apricot, clasped mine.

"Listen, my boy," said the old woman. "My sister will be able to tell you more than I ever could. She has an excellent memory, and she knows everything about everyone. Not like me: I forget everything. I wouldn't be able to go into detail. Tell her I sent you. She'll remember, she'll be able to help."

And so off we went to see Tante Augustine, Solange Lecuyer's sister. Max said he didn't know her so well, he never visited, she frightened him, she was like an old witch, he'd rather wait. But I insisted.

As we left Max's, we saw Big Berthe approaching in the distance. We hadn't heard from her in five days. When she'd jumped from the bridge, she'd jumped too far left and her knee had struck a rock before she disappeared entirely beneath the murky water. Once she resurfaced, she'd floated for a moment and, since she wasn't far from shore, managed to grab hold of a long clump of grass. She'd swallowed a lot of water, was coughing and howling in pain, and blood was gushing from her knee. We raced out of the water in a panic, threw our clothes back on, and, fishing rods under our arms, beat a hasty retreat.

Over the days that followed, since there was no sign of her in the village, we speculated that perhaps she hadn't made it out of the water, hampered by her considerable girth and the injured knee. Perhaps, exhausted after hours of calling for help, she had gone under and drowned in the river. Had she no longer been of this world, that would have been just fine by us. She wouldn't be able to say we'd talked her into jumping and then left her in the water. "She decided to jump," said Max. "No one forced her to." But that was only half true; if we hadn't been there, she wouldn't, I don't think, have risked the jump. "We would have heard if she'd died," Max added, as if to reassure himself. "There would have been a funeral."

As it happened, Berthe had survived her ordeal. She was an exceptionally strong girl. She had managed to haul herself up out of the water and, having by some miracle survived the accident, there she was, now limping toward us. She clasped her hands together and cried, "Hallelujah! Max, you owe me a smacker on the lips!" Max was having none of it, of course, but she insisted. She threatened to tell his parents everything, so Max led her into the barn and, barely thirty seconds later, they came out again, Berthe laughing her head off and Max wiping his mouth with the back of his hand. Berthe tittered as she continued on her way, pointing at us like we were idiots.

Tante Augustine's house was just as you left the village on your way to Neufchâteau. I walked backward the whole way and Max did the same. The postman passed by on his bike and stared at us, perplexed.

We knocked at Tante Augustine's door. She opened it, and before me stood a wizened old woman. Her grey hair was a mess, her eyelids were purple, and she was wearing an old-fashioned alpaca dress, a shabby blue shawl across her shoulders. She looked a little like Colette, the writer. We'd seen photos of her in class and studied a few of her short stories.

"It's Max. Max Bartroz. Grand-mère Solange sent us."

"Little Max, come in! It's so nice to have visitors. Come in, children."

We walked into the kitchen, which had a dirt floor. A bare bulb dangled from the ceiling and sticky, ochre fly paper hung from the beams; dozens of trapped flies twitching in the throes of death. The place smelled of onion, garlic, potatoes, and cold cooking oil. To the right, there was a small window with yellowed curtains and a big worm-eaten dresser. To the left: a huge pot over the fire and, at the back of the room, a broad glass-panelled armoire containing a collection of dolls, although they looked more like rags or gnarled root vegetables vaguely reminiscent of the human form.

Tante Augustine had us sit on a bench and brought us biscuits that were stale and had an aftertaste of boiled cabbage.

The old woman sat opposite us in a large armchair and adjusted her shawl.

I clasped my hands together in my lap like a good boy.

"Tante Augustine, Émile would like to clear up a few details about his parents."

"Émile? Émile who?"

"Émile Claudel," said Max.

"Ah, the little fox! So, what would you like to know, young man?" she asked, turning to me.

"I've heard a rumour that my father isn't my father."

"Ah yes, well..."

She hesitated.

"Would you like another biscuit?" she asked, trying to distract us.

"No, no," said Max, making a face.

"No thank you," I said, feebly.

There was a long silence.

At last, Max said:

"We won't stay long. We just wanted to find out a few things."

"So, well..." she said, clearing her throat. "Well, people say a lot of things. Of course, I know all about the village because I've lived here since I was born. So, young man," she said, taking my hand. "They say your papa was an American, a G.I."

"A G.I.?" I said, my eyes widening.

"Yes. Let me explain. It was early September 1944. The villagers, like those in all the other towns in our valley, had taken cover. Some were hiding in cellars, others in hastily dug trenches. They said we were about to be liberated. We'd been waiting for that day for so long, but it never seemed to come. Paris had been liberated on August 25, though, so it would only have been, if all went well, a matter of days, and indeed the Americans did come. Mayerville was liberated on September 13, 1944, one day after Neufchâteau. We were so happy, but we were still on our guard: it was still dangerous. The Germans had retreated to the woods and were still fighting fiercely. A G.I. was sent to stay at your mother's house. He'd been wounded. A German had shot him as he was pushing the enemy east. Your mother looked after him. The army camp wasn't far. The wounded stayed with the locals, it happened all the time. The G.I.—what was his name? Jack? Joe? Jim? I can't remember—stayed with your mother for a few months. They've been sending each other letters for years. Your mother, my dear Émile, kept in touch with him all this time. She must have so many letters. Other soldiers went on to Nancy, but he stayed back with your mother, nice and cozy. I still have newspapers from back then in the cellar. They describe how the Americans won control of the region. Would you like to see them?"

"No, it's OK," Max said, smiling.

"One day, it was November or December 1944, late 1944, in any case, I went to visit your mother. We don't see each other anymore, a dispute over money, a loan that was never repaid, I'll spare you the details. I was looking for my son everywhere that day, and since he was friends with your brother Michel, I went there looking for him. I went in through the barn. I knocked on the kitchen door, but there was no answer. I knew very well your mother was home. Where else could she be? It was winter, freezing cold, she couldn't have been in the garden, she wouldn't have gone out. So, I opened the door and went into the kitchen. There were two glasses on the table, a half-empty carafe of red wine, and, on one of the chairs, the G.I.'s jacket. I assumed they'd gone off to one of the bedrooms. There wasn't a sound in the house. Your father, of course, was in Germany. He'd been captured at the very start of the war.

"But that doesn't prove a thing," I said, defensively.

"Maybe not. But what's curious about the whole story is that you were born mid-November."

"November 22," I said, surprised that she knew the month.

"And your father," she went on, "wasn't released until the war was over. I saw him come back home with all the others, at any rate. Some prisoners came home earlier, but not many. Look, I have a photo from back then."

She stood up and went into her bedroom to rummage around in one of the dresser drawers. We could hear her wheezing and muttering to herself. She returned holding a photo.

"See?" she said. "This photograph was taken outside of your house, my little fox. That's your mother; her elderly parents; a friend of the family, Jacques Reims; Ducal, your neighbour from across the road, who used to own your house; and me and my friend Lulu Guillemin. Joseph Claudel is nowhere to be seen, you'll notice!"

She handed me the photo, then added:

"And what's the date on the back?"

"April 21, 1945," I said shyly.

"But that doesn't prove a thing!" Max protested, grabbing the photo. "Perhaps Joseph Claudel took the photograph!"

"Not at all," said Tante Augustine. "It was my sister Solange who took the photograph!"

The old woman got up, went to spit in the sink, and sat back down.

"Joseph Claudel was as thin as a rake when he came back at the end of May," she went on. "He'd eaten nothing but bad bread and rutabagas in the stalag. He had trouble swallowing. He practically had to learn how to chew all over again. Your mother was very patient. She was always by his bed."

She stopped and hawked up more phlegm.

"So, your father came home with the others in May 1945 and you, my boy, you were born on November 22!

Don't you know it takes nine months for a child to come into this world?"

"Of course we do," said Max, rolling his eyes.

"When did the G.I. leave?" I asked. "Was he still there in 1945?"

"I just don't know anymore, son."

Max counted on his fingers.

"That means the American stayed at the Claudels' until at least February, right?"

The old woman thought for a while.

"Yes, around then."

She scratched her head in silence.

We looked at her quizzically. She seemed to hesitate.

"But now that I think of it, the G.I. didn't stay until February 1945. He can't have. He left with his regiment once he was all better, or perhaps a little after that, but he certainly wasn't still in the village at Christmas. He might even have been gone by All Saints' Day."

"So, let's say," said Max, "that the soldier had already left by January or February 1945. Then who might Émile's father be if it's not the G.I. and it's not Joseph Claudel?"

She thought for a moment.

"Well, then," she said, scratching her nose. "Perhaps Louis Ducal."

I was speechless. Ducal, to my mind, was a bully, a sadist, a man who was more like Prince Paulo the Tyrant than a father figure.

"He and your mother were very close," the old woman continued. "They say Ducal sold her the house for next to nothing, as if he were doing her a favour. But your mother has always been... popular, let's just say. She gets on very well with the gentlemen. She's on very good terms, for example, with her gardener, and even with the priest."

Max looked at me, embarrassed.

"So, what you're saying," said Max, "is that Émile's father could just as easily be the gardener or even the parish priest?"

"But the priest is barely twenty!" I protested, before Tante Augustine could reply.

"He looks young, but he's not that young!" she exclaimed. "One thing's for certain, my dear, and that's that your sister Chantal isn't your father's daughter. She's the Gypsy's. Everyone knows that."

I leapt to my feet. It was all too much. My ears were ringing, I was sweating, and feeling so faint I had to lean against the wall so as not to fall. Without a thought, I rushed down a dark hallway and found myself standing before the door that led out into the garden. I pushed it open, went to sit on a rock, and began to sob. Max came out and gave me a little pat on the back, telling me not to worry.

"I don't want Ducal to be my father," I sniffed. "If I had to choose, I'd rather it was the G.I."

We played for a while in the garden, dunking our heads in the rain barrel and seeing who could stay under the longest. On my third go, I stayed underwater for so long that Max began to get worried. "Émile! Émile!" he shouted and he yanked me up by my shirt collar, but I held on to the barrel's sides with both hands. "Stop fooling around," Max said, indignantly. Abandoning myself to a strange sensation of hopelessness, I decided not to resurface. By the time my head at last came up out of the water, I was gasping for breath and my eyes were filled with tears and rainwater. "Your face is completely blue," Max said disapprovingly. My lips began to move in silence. I was shivering. "Come on," said Max. "Let's go back in."

We went back inside Tante Augustine's house. She had fallen asleep on a chair by the stove, her head resting against the wall, and she was snoring. We tiptoed across the kitchen. We opened the door, which woke the old woman. She leapt to her feet and shouted, "Leaving so soon? Take some biscuits with you!" But we were long gone.

PART II

*And he fixed a thoughtful gaze upon the little fox
imprisoned there, with staring coat, within his own
four walls, darting frightened glances here and there to
see whether he could find some way of escape.*

François Mauriac, translated by Gerard Hopkins,
A Woman of the Pharisees

1.

I was sitting on a deck chair in the garden when my mother, looking haggard, dark shadows under her eyes and a deep line between her eyebrows that disfigured her face, came and stood in front of me.

"Did you go out this morning?" she asked after a while.

"Yes. I mean... no."

She ran her right hand over her bare arm, then scratched her ear.

"Did you go out or not? Tell the truth!"

"Yes, I went out."

I stood, ready to run off, but she grabbed the collar of my shirt and dragged me close.

She stank of cigarettes and ammonia.

"Where did you go?" she shouted, shaking me.

"To Max's, as usual."

"I told you not to go out."

"Wasn't that yesterday?"

"This morning, too."

She let go of my collar, then slapped me around the head with her right hand.

"And where did you go after that?"

"Nowhere. I came home."

"Don't lie to me. You went over to old Augustine's, didn't you?"

"Yes... maybe..."

She glowered at me and tilted her head to one side.

"I forbid you from going to see that old gossip."

"She's Max's aunt."

"I don't care if she's Max's aunt. Do you know what type of woman she is, that old hag?"

I pouted and took a step back, ready to make my escape, but she grabbed my hair and pulled hard.

"Come with me," she said furiously.

She shoved me ahead of her, kicked me up the backside, and steered me inside into the hall. We went up the steep wooden staircase and I stopped halfway. I leaned on the banister and turned around.

"Why are you so mean?" I demanded.

She screamed with rage and slapped me.

"Come on, up!"

She pushed me up to the landing, bundled me into my room, and followed me over to my bed. She made me lie on it.

"You're not going out again until I say so!" she shouted, then she stormed out and locked the door behind her.

2.

Three days later, a Thursday, I went to the presbytery for catechism. I arrived ahead of time, something that occurred so seldom that it bears mentioning. When I went inside, the parish priest was sitting in the dark, on a straw chair in front of the fireplace, his head tipped forward, his hands on his knees. The room smelled of incense and stew.

"Father," I said very quickly, "are you my father, Father?"

He lifted his head, forehead creased and eyes wide.

"What? Your father? How do you mean?"

"Uh... my papa?"

"Your papa is Joseph Claudel, you fool! You only have one father!"

"I asked because I'm not sure my father really is my father."

"Whatever makes you think that?"

I couldn't help but notice the beads of sweat pearling on his forehead.

"Rumours. In the village. People say—"

"Whatever are you on about?"

I stayed quiet.

"Lying is a sin, my boy. Spreading loathsome gossip is also a sin."

I still didn't speak.

"You'll have to confess."

"I haven't done anything wrong, Father. That's just what I've heard. I didn't ask anything. I'm sure my father isn't my father."

"*My father isn't my father*, what nonsense!" the priest exclaimed. "It's as though you were to say, *I am not me, I am another*. It makes no sense."

"Yes, it does," I said, because I had to say something.

"You always have an answer for everything," he said, sighing theatrically. "You never stop talking, and you say the first thing that pops into your head."

He stood and wagged a finger at me.

"Careful, my boy. That can get you in hot water! You'll have to learn to keep your thoughts to yourself, to hold your tongue, and to speak only at the right time. Do you understand? You don't think before you speak. It'll get you into trouble."

"I can't stand silence."

"Sometimes it takes a little silence if words are to have an impact. Otherwise they don't stand out. Words have force only when used in moderation, and when they are to the point. Do you see?"

I began to cry. All the talk had upset me. The priest came up to me and held me tight. He smelled of sweat and incense. I could have stayed there, pressed against his belly, for hours. He tousled my hair and patted my back. After a moment, he took me by the shoulders, then grabbed my hands and squeezed them hard.

"Come, young man. Don't fret, and pay no heed to the rumours."

The other boys arrived for catechism and we all went into the back room.

3.

You run naked through the forest. You roll around in the dirt, covered in leaves. It starts to rain. You take shelter under a tree. You shiver.

4.

It was raining in Mayerville and it was cold. And yet it was summer. Max and his family had gone to Alsace to stay with his cousins. Violent storms broke, torrential rain beat down for days on our little village and the surrounding countryside. The rain poured across roof tiles, spilled out of drainpipes, causing the stream and the Vair to swell; to everyone's surprise, the river was almost in spate. The fog lingered long into the morning. Clothes refused to dry indoors. The swallows took cover. Children played checkers, ludo, and rummy. They were bored. After a few days, unable to sit still anymore, tired of being shut up, they went outside, splashed around in the puddles, sheltered under the trees. And then, one Tuesday, the fine weather returned. And soon a heatwave followed and the summer went on as it had begun, all stifling heat and glorious sunshine.

5.

What was the American soldier's name? Was he still alive? What happened to him after he left my mother's house? I wanted to know. I had to find a way to get a hold of the key to the loft where my mother kept her old things, because that's where she stored the letters and document, which—I was more convinced than ever since Tante Augustine had said that my mother and he had been corresponding for years—would shed light on the G.I.'s identity and, at the same time, my father's.

One day, as I was hiding behind a curtain where I'd been waiting, perfectly still, since that morning, I saw my mother, looking wan, a stray lock of hair falling down over her forehead, come into the living room and make her way to the hearth. From the mantelpiece, she picked up, glancing left and right all the while, a tin of dragées, doubtless a gift from some long-forgotten wedding, that I had never noticed before. She opened it, plunged a hand into the immaculate candy, and pulled out a key.

6.

Miraculous key. Symbolic key. Celestial key. Earthly key. Magical key. Key to my every desire.

7.

My mother left the living room. I tiptoed after her. She went up into the loft. I spied on her from my crouched position at the top of the stairs. My mother went over to a little trunk that held stacks of letters. She dropped in it a letter she'd been carrying in her pocket, that had no doubt just arrived, and began to read some of the older letters, a blissful smile gradually giving way to a pained expression. She wiped her face on her sleeve and sniffled. She refolded the letters and put them back in the trunk. As soon as she stood up, I left my hiding place and soundlessly made my way back down the stairs.

8.

The days dragged by.

I was bored.

I amused myself capturing bluebottles in little black ashtrays on the kitchen table. The upside-down ashtrays would trap the flies for a second or two before they escaped through the short tunnel formed by the ciga-rette rest. Drawn to the light, the flies effortlessly made their escape and flew off.

I couldn't wait for Max to come back.

I needed help with my plan.

9.

I passed the time as best I could. One morning I went to see Laurice Mahler. Her black eyes, her black bowl cut, her black eyebrows... She had a strange, wild beauty to her that unsettled me. Her house was falling in around her. The shutters had come away from the windows and just lay there in the mud. A pane that had been smashed one raucous evening had been covered over with cardboard, the glass never replaced. The kitchen walls were black with soot and grease. Laurice's mother, who never left the house, would sit all day in a chair by the window. Her father had died of cirrhosis, and her brother, who was only a few years older than her, had become head of the household. The brother had had a very strange childhood. When he was two, he'd gone missing in the woods and it had taken four years to find him. He'd been found crouched by a pond, growling like an animal and clutching a filthy old doll that was missing a leg. People said he'd survived only because a she-wolf or some other animal had protected him in the forest. When her son was returned to her, Madame Mahler had fallen to her knees, her arms outstretched like a cross. After his time in the wild, the child no longer spoke. He had to learn how to talk all over again. He wasn't toilet trained and ran off more than once, but within a few years he was once again part of village life, and a nearly normal child. I say "nearly normal," since he would fly into rages of incredible violence at the slightest provocation. People said he would beat his mother and sister during those fits of anger. Their arguments were the stuff of legend. Pots, pans, plates, and glasses would go flying out the window and land in the road. People laughed, people made fun of them, but as they cast aspersions, I could also detect a vague sadness in their eyes, a compassion they were determined to hide at any cost.

Laurice asked me to follow her into her bedroom, a tiny room at the back of the stable, with a makeshift bed atop the straw. "Don't worry, my brother isn't in," she said. "Sit." And she kneeled before me and pressed her lips to mine. Her mouth was a strawberry, a gumdrop. Then she removed her lips from mine and shuffled back. "We're going for a picnic," she said, picking herself up. "Wait for me here. I'll get us something to eat." After a few minutes, I was still waiting so I lay back and fell asleep, my head propped against the wall. A teasing laugh woke me a few minutes later. I opened my eyes with a yawn. "I leave you alone for five minutes and you take a nap?" She was holding a large jute bag. "Bread, cheese, hard-boiled eggs," she said. "Let's go."

We left the house, walked along the road, then took a path, the Chemin de la Croix. We found a spot in a meadow. Laurice spread out an old, scratchy blanket, and we sat cross-legged, facing each other. She took the food out of her bag and we ate in silence.

"You're very quiet," she said, sounding irritated.

I didn't know what to say. She intimidated me.

"I got us a surprise for dessert," she announced.

She produced two slices of bread and butter and sprinkled cocoa on top.

After our little feast, she sighed and began to undress. "It's so hot," she murmured, lying down on the blanket in only her underclothes. Her knees were grazed and she had brown splotches on her arms. Her damp body smelled like an overripe watermelon. "Come lie down," she laughed. "I'll show you something."

I lay down. She lifted her hips and slipped off her panties, throwing them onto the grass. She spread her legs a little. What struck me most was her pubic hair, even up to her belly.

She told me to take off my clothes. I hesitated. She insisted.

I got undressed very slowly. I don't know if I was afraid or if it was something we'd eaten, but suddenly my stomach ached. Once I was completely naked, she reached over and stuck her tongue in my mouth, then, with an expert hand, she took hold of my limp penis. She tried to rouse it, but it remained as soft as a slug, and after five minutes, since she was getting tired, she removed her tongue from my mouth, which was by now quite sore from her intense kisses, and jumped to her feet. She picked up her things and, without a word, disappeared.

10.

You are, at night's end, on all fours in the dust on the path behind the house, and then in a field by the woods. You run, you run until you're out of breath. The smell of cowpats and wild mushrooms in the air, the sound of a fountain, the moon in all its glory, you are happy and unhappy. You are laughing and crying. Your coarse fur, your coat the colour of dead leaves, damp from the dew, your little body and your little muscles, the iris of your eyes dilated, heart beating, tongue hanging out, you run and run until you can't breathe anymore.

11.

Meals at home were torture. My mother and Chantal would pick at their food; my father would eat slowly and chew loudly, much to my exasperation; and Michel devoured everything put in front of him. My mother would sit stiffly. Contemptuous and uncompromising, she'd watch me out of the corner of her eye, staring at my hands. My father never said a word. He'd wipe his plate clean with his bread for minutes at a time and even dip his bread into the serving dish. Michel would have a napkin tucked into his collar, but his shirt and pants would be splattered with grease. Chantal would cover her plate, still half full, with her gingham serviette, seemingly disgusted. She'd pour herself a half glass of wine, which she'd water down. My mother, growing more hostile by the minute, would sigh loudly. I wanted one thing and one thing only: to be excused.

12.

Max was back. It was a beautiful sunny day. We set out for Domrémy-la-Pucelle, a twelve-kilometre walk away, with a bag full of ham, hard-boiled eggs, a banana, and bread for lunch. We visited the house where Joan of Arc once lived, and then the basilica. I thought I heard voices as I walked into the dark, icy nave. Someone whispered, "My son, come to me. I've found you at last." I shivered. I could sense a presence in front of the altar. Someone or something brushed against my cheek.

I hurried outside. Max came running after me, asking what was going on. "I don't like this place," I told him.

We picnicked on the grass, and before we headed back to Mayerville we stopped by the souvenir shop, where I bought a set of rosary beads and Max a figurine of the Maid of Orleans. As the lady was giving him his change, I stole a box of matches and two postcards.

Just before we got to Mayerville, we spotted an abandoned old barn, surrounded by meadow. We rested for a while in the shade behind it. Before we went on our way, I took out the box of matches and asked Max, "If we set fire to the barn, do you think it would burn down to the ground?"

"I don't know."

"Shall we try?"

We gathered together some twigs and straw and piled them against the side of the building. I struck a match on the red phosphorous strip and threw it into the barn between two boards, then I lit another right after that and dropped it onto the pile of twigs and straw. I motioned to Max to step back. The fire took right away. Flames flickered in the breeze and were soon licking at the sides of the wooden barn. I held my breath. Max's eyes were black as night. I grabbed him by the arm and we ran east as fast as our legs could carry us. Once we reached the top of the hill, we turned and watched the barn burning in the distance, amazed at so much beauty, then surprised and shocked at our daring.

13.

On my way home, I cut across the church square, where I saw my sister Chantal and her friend Rachel sitting by the fountain, skirts hiked up and feet in the water. I could see my sister's panties. Standing in front of her, the Gypsy's eyes gleamed, his arms crossed and a Gauloise hanging from the corner of his mouth. I watched all three of them for a moment. They were telling stories, laughing. Chantal ran her tongue across her lips, a hand in her hair as she eyed the Gypsy's muscles. I walked up and said to Chantal, "Careful, he might be your father. I wouldn't flirt, if I were you." My sister pretended not to hear. Her friend looked at me in fright. The Gypsy lunged at me, arms out as if he were ready to strangle me. I stuck out my tongue and ran to the top of the village.

14.

"How would you like to go see a dead woman?"

"What dead woman?"

"Madame Dumont. She died yesterday."

The Dumonts lived beside the bar and tobacco store. We walked there backward. Max knocked at the door. The daughter, her face looking drawn since she'd no doubt been up all night, opened it.

"We've come to say our goodbyes to Madame Dumont."

"Did you know her well?"

"She always used to give us candy," said Max. "Sometimes she'd invite us in."

"She was very kind," I added, sadly.

"Come in, then. It's at the end of the hall."

She disappeared off into the kitchen, where other family members were sitting around the table, a glass of red wine in hand.

At the end of the hall, we reached a darkened room. I went over to the bed, where the dead woman was lying. She was holding a set of rosary beads. Max stayed back. The old woman's body was covered in gauze, but a bluebottle had worked its way in underneath and was crawling across her puffed-up face, sometimes on her nose—might it go up one of her nostrils?—sometimes on a closed eyelid or across her waxy forehead.

We often went to see the dead at their wakes. It gave us something to do. There were the good-looking ones, the ones who died smiling, who seemed to merely be sleeping, whose skin retained its glow; but there were also the graceless ones, whose pain at the moment they passed away could be read on their faces, those you could tell were sad to have left, those whose skin had turned yellow, brown, or black.

I reached out and touched the sole of the dead woman's foot. The lifeless flesh was firm and ice-cold.

15.

The next day at noon, my mother was in a foul mood. My parents had been arguing. About money, I think. They weren't talking. They wouldn't even look at each other. My mother had prepared a meal of endives with a dead bird I didn't know the name of. "Gérard's been out hunting," she said, all of a sudden. I didn't understand: it definitely wasn't hunting season. My parents chewed on the animal flesh that was full of lead shot, pretending not to notice every time it went crunch. I spat onto my plate the chunks I'd chewed on without managing to swallow. My mother smacked me on the back of the head, scooped up the half-chewed mouthfuls in her harpy fingers, and shoved them into my mouth. Tears streamed down my cheeks. I had no choice but to swallow them whole, pieces of cold, masticated meat that tasted of death.

16.

That afternoon on my way into the kitchen, I came across the newspaper for the region. It lay open on page 3 on the Formica table. There was an article about a fire in a barn and there was apparently some debate as to whether it had been an accident or deliberate. A farmer who had been resting inside the barn had been found burned to death.

Suddenly my mother came into the kitchen. I closed the newspaper. I couldn't move for the longest time. My mother was speaking to me, but I wasn't listening. I bit down on the inside of my cheek, muttered something incomprehensible, and rushed out of the room with the firm intention of never setting foot there again.

17.

That evening, my mother was chatting on the patio with a neighbour. They were talking about me. I was hiding behind a privet. I didn't dare go back inside. "He's insufferable," my mother lamented. "He gives me such a hard time. He's unruly, ungrateful, rude, impolite, ill—" She'd been about to say "ill bred," I think, but she caught herself in time.

I slipped inside and up to my room. I read *The Three Musketeers* for an hour, then went back down for supper. My father was saying that a barn had burned down not far from the village and that the police suspected foul play. "It was in this morning's newspaper," my mother said. I chewed my meat without managing to swallow, desperately wishing I could spit it all out. My father said they weren't talking about the same barn. "The one in the paper, where the man died, that was closer to Neufchâteau. The one I'm talking about was on the outskirts of the village. No one died there."

I stuffed a piece of bread in my mouth and almost choked. My sister slapped me hard on the back, taking the opportunity to wallop me as hard as she could. My mother rolled her eyes. Since there was no dessert, I asked to be excused and went up to my room. I lay down on the bed, hands behind my head, and shut my eyes, relieved to hear that I wasn't a murderer after all. After a few minutes, I fell asleep, still fully dressed.

Around three o'clock in the morning, I heard my brother Michel come in drunk. He was struggling to climb the stairs, and was raving incoherently all the while. My mother got up and went to him. She whispered, "Come into the kitchen." I got up as well and went down the stairs, making sure they didn't creak. My mother had just closed the kitchen door. I peered through the keyhole and saw my brother clinging unsteadily to the back of a chair with one hand and, with the other, holding a tin bowl that he was vomiting into. His shoes and the hems of his pants were covered in blood. His shirt was torn. It wasn't the first time my brother had come home daubed in blood and mud, his face black and blue as if he'd been fighting. He'd say he'd gone to a dance or to the carnival in a neighbouring village. He'd come home in a drunken stupor, crying like a little boy and calling for our mother from the barn, where he'd stumbled and couldn't get up. "France, come rescue me," he'd shout. He always called her France, whereas my sister and I, and even our father, only ever called her Maman.

18.

"Maman," a word that doesn't sit well in my mouth, a phatic term I use out of habit, but whose real meaning eludes me.

19.

Another dead woman. Someone had put coins over her eyelids and a towel beneath the chin to keep her mouth shut. Her lips were a purplish blue and her nose, violet. "It's important to keep watch over our dead," said Max.

20.

Fed up with never getting any dessert, I decided to pay a visit to my father's bakery and sample his delicacies for myself. Since I had a copy of the key, it wasn't hard, when night came, to slip inside the store. I went in the back way, down a dark alley. I turned the key in the lock. I went inside without turning the lights on. Even though I rarely went there—I'd never been welcome—I knew my way around. I knocked over a jug in the darkness. I threw myself at the pastries, eating fifteen cream puffs, three éclairs, four brioches, three raisin buns, two lemon tarts, and five mille-feuilles, and, on my way out, after carefully locking the door behind me, I had to dash behind the church, where I vomited into a ditch.

21.

You wake with a start, hair soaking wet, pyjamas sticking to your skin, blood pounding at your temples like a drum. In your dream, your brother Michel has turned into a wolf and you, the little fox, are absolutely terrified. The wolf asks you to follow it, and you do so reluctantly. You reach the banks of the Vair. The wolf says, "Look, look in the water." At first you can see nothing but the full moon reflected in the river, but as you look closer, you can make out, just beneath the surface, the half-rotted corpses of children floating like plastic dolls, hands joined like a series of paper figurines. The wolf says, "Look! Behold my handiwork!" There is unspeakable suffering in the children's eyes; it's all too much, so you run away, leaving behind the wolf, who begins to howl.

22.

The night bled, the day cried.

23.

I went off to find the collection of poems I had stolen from my brother one day and hidden in my tin box. At nightfall, by the light of a candle, I read the elegant lines whose meaning I did not always grasp:

Behold the sweet evening, friend of the criminal;
It comes like an accomplice, stealthily; the sky
Closes slowly like an immense alcove,
And impatient man turns into a beast of prey.

I closed the little notebook, promising myself that one day I, too, would write poetry.

24.

My mother wanted to go shopping in Neufchâteau. Since she didn't drive, the gardener took her in his old Citroën. As soon as they left, I went straight to the living room and took the key out from the bottom of the box of dragées. I motioned to Max, who was waiting in the courtyard, to follow me. We went up to the loft. Max kept watch at the top of the stairs. My sister was out. My brother was at the bakery.

My heart was beating fast. I dug around in an old trunk where I discovered bundles of letters from the G.I. who, I realized, had indeed been writing to my mother for years, just as Tante Augustine had said. I picked up a letter at random.

My dear France,
All is well here. It has been terribly hot for days now. The fan in the bedroom is broken. I'm having trouble sleeping.
I understand when you say how hard you work looking after your children and your house. It must be difficult.
I have so many fond memories. Yes, it was a strange time, for me, for all of us, there was a war on, but we lived

our lives to the fullest. Those who did not live through it cannot hope to understand. It was almost ten years ago now, and yet it feels like it were a century.

My beautiful children are growing fast. James is turning 6 and Katherine is 4.

I'm learning French in the evenings. Pour m'améliorer. J'aime beaucoup ça.

It's the same old routine with us. But we're happy.

Do the villagers have washing machines now? I can still remember the fountains. The one near you was absolutely huge. Is it still there?

I can remember your garden under all that snow, your house...

Will you come visit me one day in America?

Signed: *Jack*

On the envelope: the address and his name, John Kingston.

In his letters, which weren't quite love letters, but close to it, because even though the American wrote of his family, his job—he was an accountant with a big firm—his house, and the pleasant community on the outskirts of Philadelphia, he often mentioned and went into detail about the time he'd spent with my mother; he spoke about it like it had been a vacation, a wonderful time, recalling preposterous things that had happened during the war, how they'd laughed and laughed one night as they mimicked some of the old folks from the village, the fine wine and the good food that my mother, despite the rationing, always managed to serve up.

The American enclosed a photo of his family. They were all sitting on the steps of their Colonial-style home.

Over time, the letters became less frequent. John Kingston sent news now and again, but the correspondence between the American and my mother seemed to have lost its spark.

France,

Thank you for your last letter, the third in a week. I sure enjoy hearing from you, but Tammy is starting to ask questions. She knows who you are, of course, but she's asking why you're writing so much. I think she might be jealous. Please don't take this the wrong way, but perhaps you should write a little less often. For a little while, at least. But don't worry—I'll keep on writing you.

Jack

Max thought he heard a noise, motioned for me to hide, then relaxed: false alarm. I kept reading. Another letter.

France,

This is my first letter to you after months of silence. I'm sorry. I haven't "abandoned" you like you said in your last letter. It's not always easy for me to write so often. I have children. We've renovated part of the house, there's no

129

shortage of things to do. I got a promotion. I have lots of
work. I'll write soon.

Jack

The last letter in the trunk was dated two years earlier. Then nothing. Perhaps my mother kept the more recent letters in her bedside table, but I wasn't going to check: I had my doubts she would leave such illicit correspondence next to where her husband slept.

I didn't have time to read it all. There were dozens of postcards. I picked up the first one that came to hand: the Empire State Building and, on the back, a simple *Love from New York*, signed *Jack*. I came across a photo of him in uniform. He was very handsome. He had white teeth, a beaming, almost clownish smile, long black eyelashes that cast a shadow below his eyes like a pencil mark, little delicate ears, and a square jaw. I pocketed the photo.

I kept rifling through the trunk and found some letters my father had written from the stalag. He said that he missed Michel and Chantal and was looking forward to seeing them again. He said he was sick of peeling and eating *Kartoffeln*. He said he dreamed of taking a shower and sleeping on clean sheets.

At the bottom of the trunk, I found a bunch of wedding photos, official papers, and birth certificates, including my own. I closed my eyes. I opened my eyes. My hand was shaking. I held my breath. There was his name. Joseph Claudel, the man people called my father, had officially recognized me. I was surprised. Perhaps even a shade disappointed. "So, he *is* my father," I said out loud. But then I realized it didn't mean a thing. Maybe he had agreed to acknowledge me even though he knew the truth, or else he'd been taken in and simply imagined himself to be my father.

Suddenly Max was running toward me. His hands were in a panic. "Someone's coming," he whispered. "What? That can't be," I muttered, annoyed. His eyes turned angry. "Did you close the door?" I asked him. He nodded. We scurried over to hide in the corner of the loft.

We heard heavy feet on the stairs, the steps creaking. Then the footsteps stopped.

The door opened.

25.

I woke up in the middle of the night. Head turned toward the wall, I didn't dare open my eyes. I was sure that someone else was in the room. I heard footsteps, then breathing louder than my own over my shoulder, heavy guttural breaths. A hand brushed against the back of my neck while another tugged at the eiderdown and sheets, about to uncover my damp body. My heart was beating fast, tears streaming down my cheeks. My brother began to cough in his bed on the other side of the landing, almost choking, and the husky breath moved off, the threatening hand hovering over my body pulled back, and I lay there, awake, for the longest time, not daring to turn around and face the room.

26.

One Sunday, Jean-François Franquin, who was known to everyone in the village since he did very well at school and was even rumoured to be going to study in Paris—something that would have raised eyebrows since he was the son of penniless, uneducated farmers—was found dead in his bathtub. It was the talk of the village. His mother was sent to hospital in Neufchâteau, because she'd stopped eating and kept fainting. His father went to stay with a neighbour. People said he was suicidal and they were keeping a close eye on him.

Max and I decided to go see the body. We knocked on the door, but there was no reply, so Max grasped the latch and pushed. We walked into the kitchen, headed down a long, dark hallway, and emerged, quite by accident, beside the body. The dead teenager was right there in front of us, lying on the bed, his body covered by a shroud. On the bedside table: a dish of water and a branch from a fir tree.

We walked over to the bed. The parish priest, who had stayed by the body through the night, was sitting beside the boy, a Bible in his hands, his head down, his chin resting on his chest, snoring softly. I tried not to make the floorboards squeak, I tried not to make a sound, but Max, his nose no doubt irritated by the smell of incense, sneezed, and the priest opened his eyes.

"Ah, my children! What a pleasant coincidence," he said, clearing his throat. "I have to go out for a little while."

He stood up and set down the Bible on the chair.

"Please stay by the body for me. I won't be long."

The priest left the room.

Max walked over to the cold body.

"Do you think he's going to heaven?"

"I'm not sure. Do the drowned go to heaven?" Max asked.

"Of course they do. Unless they committed suicide. Maybe it was suicide."

"I doubt it," said Max. "Jean-François Franquin wasn't really the type to kill himself."

"Not the type? How would you know?"

"It was an accident. He fell asleep in the bath. The water was too warm, the bathroom was full of steam, I heard. He suddenly felt unwell. And drowned."

"But how can anyone die in the bath?"

Max didn't reply. He was looking at the motionless shape shrouded in white.

When he was alive, Jean-François Franquin had been very handsome: black hair, tall, muscular, his skin an aristocratic white—quite the opposite of his parents, who were short, scrawny, and bronzed.

I was curious to know what a drowned body looked like. So I drew back the shroud to the foot of the bed. Jean-François Franquin was wearing a nightshirt. His hands were folded across his chest, his belly was swollen, his face was puffy with hints of blue. His lips were gone.

Max pulled the young man's nightshirt up around his neck and we put our ears to his chest. "Perhaps I'll be a doctor one day," said Max in all seriousness. We'd never seen such a young body and our emotions got the better of us. Our first teenager.

Suddenly we heard the front door open. Max yanked the drowned boy's nightshirt back down and I threw the shroud back over him.

"Thank you, my children," the priest said as he came into the room. He sat down without looking at us and went on reading his Bible.

Since we just stayed there beside the bed, the priest raised his head and said, "You may go now." And since we still stayed rooted to the spot, he added, "Go on, out! Visiting hours are over."

27.

"How about we go poke around Ducal's house?" Max asked one day when he'd come over to see me.

Like me, Max had his doubts. The birth certificate I'd found in the loft hadn't convinced him. Max said, "Claudel said you were his son on paper, but that doesn't mean anything. It doesn't prove a thing." Max was certain we'd find out more at Ducal's. I was reluctant to say yes. I was frightened at the thought of going over there. I imagined Ducal, like Prince Paulo on his estate, living out his sadistic, perverted tendencies there. Just like Prince Paulo, Ducal probably had servants instead of furniture, sitting on them instead of chairs. I imagined him turning all his enemies into metal statues and holding them prisoner in dungeons, cages, or aquariums, young people whose suffering he'd enjoy watching as he tortured them.

Max insisted. I said yes. Perhaps we would discover some papers that would tell us more about Ducal: what did he know about the G.I.? What did he keep in his lambskin notebook? Why did our sheets have his initials on them? Why had Pim, who, as far as I knew, had no ties to him, appeared at his window? Might Ducal be my real father? And who was Ducal really, that mysterious man who seemed to be both nowhere and everywhere at once?

But how were we going to get into his house?

As luck would have it, one day I overheard him tell my mother he was off to Paris for three days on business. A few hours after he left, Max and I circled his house looking for a way in, a broken basement window we might be able to slip through. But there was nothing.

Peering down into the well behind the frightful house, the very same well where Ducal's wife had drowned herself, we realized that it was dry. A stone we tossed in confirmed there was no water. Then the idea came to me, inspired by an episode I'd read in an adventure novel, that we might take a rope and rappel our way down into the well and see if a pipe would lead us inside the house. "I suppose it's possible," said Max, making a face that betrayed his skepticism.

The following night, armed with a rope and Wonder pocket lamp that Max had brought with him, we made our way through the garden. We fastened the rope to a ring on the side of the well and eased ourselves down. There wasn't one but two pipes at the bottom: one to the left and one to the right. We'd have to decide which way to go. Max waved for me to go left. We crept through the cramped tunnel and, after a few minutes—it seemed as though they would never end; oxygen was becoming scarce and I'd worked up a sweat—we arrived at the foot of a narrow staircase. We climbed the steps, struggling not to fall, since the stone had worn away and crumbled beneath our feet. We found ourselves on a small landing at the base of another staircase that led out onto a long hallway, at the end of which we came to a half-rotten trap door. We pushed it open and found ourselves in a cellar cluttered with empty bottles, mouldy old trunks, and strange-looking iron contraptions that could conceivably have been used for torturing children. From there, it was easy enough to make our way to the ground floor of Ducal's vast home. We opened a door and found ourselves in the kitchen. My heart was beating wildly. What if someone was home?

I didn't want a repeat of the terror we'd felt the week before when Max and I had gone up into the loft to read my mother's letters and rifle through the family papers. Hidden in a corner, we had been paralyzed by fear. Someone was there. When the door opened, we saw my brother Michel appear, his face tormented, his hands in knots, his clothes filthy, as though he had been rolling around in the mud. He went over to the other side of the loft, where the old suitcases were. He opened one and took out some children's clothes, which he looked at with tears in his eyes. His body shook and he let the clothes fall to the dusty floor, all apart from a tiny winter coat that he clutched against his chest, then held up to his face as he began to sob.

We'd had to wait for my brother to finish prostrating himself before those mysterious relics and return to his room below before it was our turn to leave the gloomy loft.

Ducal's house was dank and depressing. The kitchen was spacious, as sophisticated as any restaurant kitchen, but terribly dirty. The living room was dusty and sinister. The shutters hadn't been closed and the moon lit up the room with its melancholic rays. The smell of mould, cold tobacco, and imitation scents. Shelves lined with old books (their spines ruined), mouldy old editions (Pierre Loti, *The History of Magic* by Éliphas Lévi, the complete short stories of Auguste de Villiers de L'Isle-Adam, Georges Rodenbach, Cyrano de Bergerac's *The Other World: Comical History of the States and Empires of the Moon*, which I flicked through and discovered that the narrator, after landing in New France, went on to reach the moon and, from there, a third world where everything was the opposite of our own, and where he was caged like a bird, which somehow reminded me of the story of Prince Paulo as well as *Erewhon: or, Over the Range*, the novel by Samuel Butler in which codes are inverted); huge, black velvet wall hangings on either side of the windows, masks on the wall and half-human/half-animal statues on little mahogany tables; dozens of solemn family portraits, each uglier than the last, in which it seemed Ducal appeared without exception, since his ancestors bore him a curious resemblance, even the strikingly masculine women.

In Ducal's bedroom upstairs: a large desk in the corner, the lambskin notebook right in the centre of it.

Inside it were stacks of bills, transactions with farmers in the village, receipts, accounts dating back to the war; Ducal kept a list of all kinds of business dealings between him and the locals, between the Germans and the villagers, between himself and the Germans. Among the documents, I found a lease stipulating that our house had been rented to my parents. So Ducal owned our home, and my mother and father were no more than tenants. I was flabbergasted. I'd thought they owned it. Not a word in the notebook about the G.I. No mention either of whether or not Ducal was a father. We went through the desk drawers and the other bedrooms and were getting ready to explore the loft when we heard voices downstairs. It was Ducal and our gardener. They were having a discussion about overwatered privets as they made their way upstairs.

28.

We scurried down to the kitchen using the backstairs. We headed for the cellar and back down the tunnel that led to the bottom of the well. Since we couldn't climb back out of the well—it faced the garden and Ducal could easily have caught sight of us from a window—we turned left, without knowing where we would end up.

The tunnel to the left was much longer than the one we'd just come out of. After a few minutes, we reached an intersection, where the pipe split into two again. We hesitated, then pressed on to the right and, legs shaking, gasping for breath, we stumbled out onto a small stone staircase at the far end, leading up to some sort of vestibule. We clambered up the handful of steps and pushed on a worm-eaten door. I was sure it would be locked, boarded up, but it opened easily at the touch of my trembling hand. To our great surprise, we found ourselves in a cellar, surrounded by dozens of bottles of wine and worm-eaten casks. It was very damp. There was a door at the end of the cellar. We pushed it open and found ourselves in the kitchen of the gardener who rented out the apartment beside our house. I was dumbstruck. The tunnel we didn't take must have led to the bottom of our well, which had been dry for years. That meant the cellar we'd just left was right below our patio, the one I'd never been inside, the one whose door led out onto the street.

I was in a Gaston Leroux detective novel. All those now-dry tunnels actually connected our house to Ducal's.

My head suddenly hurt and a thousand questions ran through my mind. Did Ducal ever slip into our house in the middle of the night? Was it he who came whenever there was a full moon, while I lay huddled in fear in my bed, feeling his fetid breath against my neck? Did he rendezvous with my mother in the loft or elsewhere in the house? Did she use the same tunnels to visit Ducal? Did the gardener know about the passageways that ran between both houses?

I took Max's hand. He was pale and exhausted, barely able to stand, and we left the gardener's lodgings through the front door. From the courtyard, we passed through the barn. Max went home and I crept back up to my room without a sound.

29.

Rumour had it that the carnival was coming to Mayerville. Every day I'd take a few coins from my mother's purse and put them aside for the big day. At the end of August, the first entertainers pulled up in their caravans. From my vantage point by the fountain, I watched them set up, barely able to contain my excitement. It was a carnival from another age, a heady blend of circus, fairground rides, and crowd-pleasing attractions.

On opening day, the delicious smell of waffles and doughnuts wafted across the village. Everyone turned out. The sun shone high in the sky. I took a pony ride with Max. I insisted on sitting back to front, which made the younger children laugh. My mother watched me from the far side of the square, her hand shielding her eyes from the sun. She was with Ducal and he cracked his knuckles as he approached me. He told me to stop acting the fool and to sit the right way round. Who did he think he was, I thought to myself.

Ducal insisted: "Stop fooling around!" The younger children stepped back; they were afraid of him. Just as he raised his cane to strike me, I stepped down off the pony and walked away from him. When I turned around, I watched him make his way back to my mother and the pair disappeared up to the top of the village, their bodies so close that they must have been walking arm in arm.

The heat was dreadful; everyone was in a sweat. The smell of French fries, sausage, waffles, and candy-floss, not to mention the whiff of beer and cheap red wine, floated in the air. A few children were sick into the stream, having eaten too much sugar. I didn't know which way to turn, dazzled as I was by so many possibilities, so many attractions. Max and I played all the games. We tried our luck at the raffle, each choosing a tiny scrap of paper rolled up like a cigarette. I won a teddy bear and Max, a little plastic airplane.

I didn't dare go on the bumper cars, but I tried everything else: the caterpillar ride, the pendulum boat ride, the archery game, the duck pond, where I won a special kind of soap that stops body hair growing back, which I later gave to my mother, the merry-go-round, the sack race in a field by the church, where I won again—a kit for perfect fingernails that I later gave to my sister—and, last of all, the House of Horrors, where we were promised monsters the likes of which we'd never seen and were shown, once inside the tent, various deformed animal foetuses in jars of formaldehyde, skeletons, cut-off hands (most likely rubber), then, right at the very end, a woman with no arms or legs, propped on a stool on a little platform. The poor woman's eyes shone hard with melancholy and her lips were pursed with deep resentment. Max and I circled the stand to see whether it was just an illusion, but we quickly agreed it was no such thing. Max didn't feel well. We left.

The highlight of the day was Marmol the Magician's little travelling theatre. Before the show got underway, I slipped backstage, where I saw a young boy sitting in front of a mirror putting his makeup on. I recognized him immediately: it was Pim, the young man with the knife that we'd met that day on the outskirts of the village and whom I'd seen later at Ducal's window. I watched the magician walk over to him and ask for help with his costume.

Around six thirty that night, a bell rang. Pim rang it with all his might, making an infernal racket. The show was about to begin, he cried. There were a few tickets left. Sitting in the first row, Max and I stuffed ourselves silly with candy. My mouth turned blue and Max's, purple. The children and housewives took their seats, chatting and laughing. Suddenly the spotlights were turned off and everyone went quiet. The strains of some vaguely Oriental-sounding music filled the big top. A violent beam of light appeared and the red curtain went up. The stage was empty and in shadows. Someone in the audience coughed. Several seconds went by and still nothing happened on stage. Children began to squirm in their seats.

Then, out of nowhere, and accompanied by another violent beam of light and a different piece of music, this one terrifying and operatic, dressed in solemn, somber colours, Marmol the Magician made his entrance. Cane in hand, dressed in a top hat and a black cape lined with red silk, he stood bolt upright and smiled a strange smile. He cried, "I am Marmol!" And, taking a bow, "My name is Cannabas Marmol, the incredible magician, the one and only Marmol!" He bore an uncanny resemblance to the magician Buatier de Kolta, whose photograph I'd seen in a magazine. He had a moustache, a beard, and generous sideburns. His hair was balding up top, shoulder-length at the back, and he had dark shadows beneath his eyes. The children in the audience were instantly intimidated by Marmol's histrionic voice, his superior demeanour, and his gleaming eyes.

He was sweating heavily and removed his cape and hat. Underneath the cape, he was wearing a stained, ill-fitting frock coat and, beneath that, a pair of pants with silk braiding down the sides and a shirt more yellow than white. Marmol looked around and, not knowing what to do with his cape and hat, shouted, "Dimitri!" Suddenly Pim appeared on stage as if by magic. The children jumped. The housewives brought their hands to their mouths. Pim, or Dimitri, was dressed like an Orthodox monk, only without the cross. His green hair stood on end and his makeup was nothing short of outrageous. He took the magician's cape and hat then disappeared as quickly as he had appeared, in a flash, as if he had vanished into thin air. No sooner had Marmol said "Prepare yourselves for an exceptional spectacle—a series of phenomenal performances, the likes of which you've never seen before!" than Pim, a.k.a. Dimitri, reappeared in the audience beside a young boy who took fright and clung to his mother. Pim began handing out playing cards to every child. Each card had the ace of hearts, a jack, or a queen on one side and, on the other, Marmol's photograph, his face powdered, hair slicked back, red lips curled in a mysterious smile. The card soon joined the other wonders in my tin box buried in the garden. How I envied Pim. I would so have loved to be part of the performance, too. I wished I was him.

The magician began his show with a rather hum-drum number that involved producing doves from his hat, scarves from his cane, and eggs from his hand, as if by a miracle, then, without warning, his assistant Dimitri grabbed a long knife and planted it in his neck. Blood spurted across the stage, and Marmol doubled over in pain, falling to his knees, but in a fashion that struck me as overly theatrical, no matter how real the blood appeared to be. The magician writhed on the floor. Some of the children, terrified, began to cry. Then Marmol's assistant cast a large veil in front of his master and, borrowing his magic wand, gave it a tap. It fell to the floor, revealing the conjurer who had completely recovered from his wounds, with no scar, no trace of blood, brandishing his knife in the air as though he had overcome Death itself. He signalled for his assistant Dimitri to come closer, and produced from his coat a panoply of knives of all shapes and sizes. Dimitri took a few steps forward and Marmol made an apple appear in his hand. He sliced it with one of the knives to prove that they were sharp. Marmol handed the knives to his assistant Dimitri, who retreated to the side of the stage. The magician remained impassive, striking a pose that implied he feared absolutely nothing. Dimitri took aim and fired off a knife in his direction; to everyone's surprise, the magician caught the blade in midair, unharmed. Dimitri threw the other knives, faster and faster, and each time Marmol snatched them out of the air with expert hands.

The next act left me stunned. Never in my godforsaken village could I have imagined witnessing such an illusion. The magician asked his assistant to bring him a large, coffin-like box. He removed the lid and the young man got inside. Marmol closed the lid and turned the box so that his audience could see there was nothing special about it. Then the magician seized a large saw and began sawing the box in two. In no time at all the young man's torso had been separated from his legs. He begged the magician to stop, feigning agony. "There must be two of them," Max whispered in my ear. There was, of course, some trick to it, but I was perplexed all the same, because I hadn't noticed anyone else backstage.

Suddenly Marmol's assistant came over to me. He didn't say a word, but gestured theatrically for me to join the magician on stage. I followed him and just before I went up, he whispered in my ear, "I think we've met before. I remember you." I was both delighted and alarmed at being chosen. What were they going to have me do? I saw Max chuckling. The magician beckoned me forward. He was standing imperiously in the middle of the stage, and I was very afraid. I was close enough to see that his face was ravaged by acne, his makeup was running. He smelled of sweat, stale tobacco, and rancid aftershave. I hoped he wouldn't hypnotize me. From my shirt and pants, he conjured all kinds of feminine-looking scarves, in all sorts of colours; from my pockets, he produced items that belonged to members of the audience and made me out to be a pickpocket. I turned as red as the blood spilled by a torture victim, but I was part of the game now and couldn't help clowning around a little, which drew a laugh from the children. I began walking backward on my hands and contorted my body into all kinds of positions. I felt like an exhibitionist, and rejoiced in the feeling. The magician let me perform a while; he even applauded, then tapped me on the shoulder and pushed me gently down from the stage and back to my seat.

Max snorted with laughter and said he was impressed by my cheek.

The magician suddenly shouted in his nasal, flamboyant voice, "For my next trick, I'll be needing a young girl..." He paused to wipe the sweat from his brow, then went on. "But I'll be needing a very clever young girl, the smartest of you all. Who's the cleverest among you young ladies?" Stifled laughter, humming and hawing, then a few hands went up. "You, miss, in the green dungarees. Yes, you at the back." Max and I turned around to see that the lucky girl was none other than Berthe, the girl who, thanks to us, had almost drowned in the Vair. Dimitri approached the miraculous survivor and took her by the hand. Berthe, red and beaming, her eyes moist with excitement, allowed Dimitri to lead her up to the stage, where the magician had her sit on a chair. With a wave of his magic wand, the chair began to levitate. The chair veered left, then right, across the stage. It was all very funny, since Berthe couldn't stop laughing and the public laughed along, too. What was no doubt a usually solemn routine had become ridiculous, and the magician's face betrayed a certain frustration, as though keen to bring the riotous scene to an end. He set Berthe back down and covered her in a sheet that Dimitri had brought him. Berthe didn't have time to react. We couldn't hear her any longer, as the tent filled with booming music that drowned out the laughter and, suddenly, with an expert hand, the magician whipped away the sheet and there was a chorus of oohs and aahs. Berthe was gone. The empty chair was floating by itself. No sign of the girl. Everyone had stopped laughing.

The highlight of the evening was a series of transformations, each more astounding than the last. Dimitri brought out a full-length mirror and set it in the middle of the stage. The magician stood behind it and stepped straight back out again. He'd changed into a woman. His moustache, beard, and sideburns had disappeared; his elaborate makeup glistened under the spotlights. It was the magician, all right—we could still make out his face, the shape of his head—but within a fraction of a second he'd turned into a woman. Max elbowed me and whispered in my ear, "It must be his sister. They look alike. She's not the magician. That's impossible." Marmol, or rather Marmol the woman, began to shout, "My name is Cannabas Marmol, the incredible magician, the one and only Marmol!" and he stepped back behind the mirror, re-emerging exactly as he had been before.

The younger children were speechless, while the adults frowned in consternation.

Then it was Dimitri's turn. Pim/Dimitri was a tall, lanky teenager, but when he walked behind the mirror and came out the other side, his body had changed: he had the muscles of a bodybuilder and he flexed them before the bewildered audience.

The magician invited one of the few men in the audience to come up on stage and walk behind the mirror. The man hesitated but, egged on by his wife, and perhaps hoping to find himself with the body of a Greek god, he agreed to play along. He went behind the mirror and out the other side came, to everyone's astonishment, an enormous pig. The audience roared with laughter. The pig began running around the stage in a panic. The poor animal grunted and whirled, frantically seeking an exit. Then it went back behind the mirror. It came out again in human form on the other side, but not in its original state: the man had changed into a woman.

There was no two ways about it, it was definitely him. The freshly minted Eve looked herself up and down in the mirror, flabbergasted, hand raised to her mouth. The magician asked her to take her seat. She muttered something along the lines of, "But how can it be? Won't I go back to how I was before?" The magician tapped her on the shoulder and whispered in her ear that she shouldn't worry. When the lady/gentleman sat back down, his/her wife and children looked on, not knowing whether to laugh or cry. I looked around and saw that Berthe still wasn't back. Her seat was empty: she'd disappeared.

The curtain fell and the audience sighed in relief after such an outpouring of emotion, such drama, then began to applaud wildly. People eventually filed out of the tent, still discussing the show among themselves. Max and I stayed for as long as we could. We were curious. Would Berthe reappear backstage? Was the man/woman in cahoots with the magician? Was he on his way to get changed backstage as we spoke? Would Marmol's second accomplice, the man involved in the casket act, put in an appearance and begin sweeping the floor clean of candy wrappers and paper tissues? We were the only audience members left when the ticket seller came into the tent and kindly asked us to leave. And so our questions remained unanswered, but we quickly forgot them. A light show was getting underway at the church square, featuring a performance by a tightrope walker. He played all kinds of instruments as he balanced on his high wire between the church and the town hall. He even offered to carry the more fearless children on his shoulders. I volunteered, of course, insisting that he carry me backward, but he refused.

Later, once the festivities had come to an end and calm had returned to the village, I spotted Marmol in the street as I walked home. To be more accurate, I smelled him before I saw him—a vague smell of rot, cigars, and opium. He was still wearing his magician's costume and staggered as though he'd been drinking. "I am Marmol!" he cried. He broke off to throw up in the little stream that ran beside the road. "My name is Cannabas Marmol, the incredible magician, the one and only Marmol!" Madame Franquin, who lived opposite, opened her shutters and told him to be quiet. Pim followed his master, dragging a large suitcase behind him. I saw Marmol and Pim go into Ducal's house. They didn't even knock, just pushed on the door and disappeared into the darkness of the hall.

30.

The next evening was August 15, the feast of the Assumption. There were fireworks at the Potelon. All the family was there: Michel, Chantal, my father, my mother. The Bartroz family was there, too: the father, the mother, Max, Julien, and little Marie. There was a refreshment stall. People from the village and environs came by the dozen. I quickly got swallowed up by the crowd. When the fireworks died down, the darkness was all-encompassing. I thought I saw Marmol the Magician—or was it Ducal?—behind me in the shadows, spying on me. The man in black approached. I felt his breath on the back of my neck. He murmured something in my ear—words in a foreign language I didn't understand. Soon I felt the man's fingers against my neck, on my ears, in my hair. Then suddenly it was as though the trees had enveloped me, their branches winding themselves around me. I was a prisoner of the forest, I could no longer escape. It was as though I'd awoken from one bad dream only to find myself in another. I was suddenly beside a pond on the edge of the woods, and the hands of the gardener, Gérard Thiebaut, were tight around my neck. "This time I've got you, you crafty thing," he whispered. "You won't get away this time." But I did manage to free myself from his clutches and I ran as fast as I could toward the village. Glancing back to see if he was following me, I saw him lift a rifle to his shoulder and take aim. He fired once, twice, then all was silent.

31.

One evening, as I was out running along dusty, forgotten paths, I spotted a silhouette in the distance, a man or a woman, holding a crying child by the hand, and they moved off across the fields and into the dusk. The sky was purple with touches of mauve, and in the air there floated the smell of cowpats and of plums that lay rotting in the grass.

32.

My tin box had disappeared.

I scraped, I kicked up the dirt, I dug deeper: nothing. Someone had been digging where the little cross marked the spot.

I searched the house from top to bottom, and finally discovered my box among many other dusty boxes underneath my brother's bed. I went to find him and threatened to reveal the truth about him. "What truth? What are you talking about?" he said. "You kill animals," I replied. "You come back home covered in blood, you hang around young children." He gave me back the box and I buried it in the same place, certain that he wouldn't dig it up again.

33.

I would have liked to hate my mother, but I could never quite bring myself to. Sometimes I'd find her in the kitchen, sitting on a stool and weeping silently. I'd say, "Whatever's wrong, Maman?" And she'd reply, "I don't know." Then she would reach out her hand so that I'd come closer. I'd hesitate. She'd grab my arm and pull me onto her lap. She smelled of sweat, naphthalene, and incense paper. She'd stroke my hair and press her moist lips to my forehead. She'd tell me to get up, then she'd go to the dresser and fetch a small tin of bergamots, the deliciously fragrant candies from Nancy, which she'd open glumly before coming back to me, her cheeks sagging, her forehead creased with wrinkles, and she'd place a few candies in the palm of my hand, whispering into my ear, "Off you go now, child. I love you, in spite of everything, you know."

34.

You see your mother going up into the loft. Her head's down, she looks deflated. You follow her. She drags her feet as she makes her way to the far end below the eaves, where you've not yet ventured because it's too dark. Your mother is swallowed up by the darkness. You hear her crying. You hesitate for a moment. You should go back to your room, but instead you continue through the darkness and there she is, on her knees, one hand covering her mouth and the other reaching out to a hideous shape in the corner, an eight-legged monster with the tail of a rat and the mouth of a whale, a mouth that it opens imploringly, like a starving baby bird. The stench is unbearable and you struggle not to vomit. Your mother is petting the thing as she cries. She hugs the beast and soon it purrs and falls asleep, then your mother stands and goes back down to the kitchen. You follow her like this every evening. As the days pass, the monster grows. Your mother feeds it table scraps. The frightful creature looks fit to burst, so swollen is it with fat and tissue. Soon its skin begins to crack, giving way to bright red flesh. The beast is at death's door, and your mother cries and stuffs her fist into her mouth so as not to scream.

35.

One Tuesday morning Max's mother was surprised to discover that the postman had slipped the letters underneath the door instead of leaving them in the letterbox as he usually did. She was passing through the hall when she saw a letter skidding across the tiles. Madame Bartroz opened the door and immediately noticed that the letterbox had gone. She went to call out to the postman, but he had already disappeared off down the street. At the very same moment, her next-door neighbour came outside to find that her letterbox had also disappeared. The women, many of whom were dressed in black or wearing a housedress and head-scarf, walked out to the road one by one. Hands on hips or arms crossed, they began talking, wondering what might have happened. The mayor was sent for, though he complained of having more important matters to attend to, and they scratched their heads and went off to look for the damned letterboxes.

They were found later that day, spread out across the grass at the Potelon. They were all there; not a single one was missing. The problem everyone immediately faced was how to identify each person's letterbox. There was not always an owner's name and, though some instantly recognized their own by some distinguishing mark—a sticker in the corner, an unusual colour, a distinctive shape—others had great difficulty identifying their own particular letterbox, and the arguing went on until very late into the night, until, eventually, tired and upset, the good people, not wanting to return home empty-handed, picked up the first letterbox that came to hand and went home.

My mother immediately came up to my room and asked, "Are you behind this?" I was lying on my bed, hands behind my head. "I don't know what you're talking about," I said. She screwed up her eyes as though trying to read my mind. "Own up now and you'll be spared the mother of all punishments. Or don't and you'll live to regret it, my friend. You can't say I didn't warn you." I rolled over, resting my head against the wall, and said very calmly, "I didn't do it." She turned and walked out of the room, slamming the door behind her.

It had been a master stroke. Max and I had arranged to meet at two in the morning, near the fountain at the foot of the Chavée. He had snuck out his bedroom window, landing in the courtyard before slipping out through the barn. I went down the steep staircase that led to the front door. It was far from my parents' room, and Michel was snoring. I'd borrowed the gardener's wheelbarrow and, each armed with a hammer and screwdriver, Max and I had walked away with virtually every letterbox in the village. It hadn't been difficult. Often the letterboxes only had to be unhooked. If they were too firmly attached to the wall or door, we let them be, a little disappointed, but the wheelbarrow was filling up and time was of the essence. The night was warm, shooting stars streaked across the sky, the streets were empty, the silence was absolute.

When we got to the Potelon, we unloaded our haul and spread it out on the grass. We were a little scared, I think, but more than anything we found the whole thing hilarious. I felt as though I didn't really know if what I was doing, if what I'd just done, was real or only a dream, trapped as I was between two places and times: on the one hand, there was a world where I hadn't been a complete idiot and, on the other, a world where we'd pulled off our daring heist with cunning and aplomb.

36.

People talked about the letterbox heist all summer long. They found it amusing because it wasn't really a heist; the stolen goods had been found easily enough, but they wondered who had done it all the same.

The rest of the summer was like the two before, full of joy and laughter. Max and I ran about everywhere, getting away with as much foolishness as we could. But then the summer ended. The Bartrozes went back to Paris. It was an awkward goodbye. The Panhard was parked by the side of the road, Monsieur Bartroz behind the wheel. Julien got into the car and gave me a wave. Little Marie came out of the house with her mother and ran over to me. "See you next year!" she said. She handed me a wool scarf that she'd knitted with her mother's help. "It's for you... for winter." Then she got into the car with her mother. Max came over to me and went to kiss me on both cheeks but pulled back at the last second. He shook my hand instead, and suddenly I felt very old indeed. "Summer's over," he said simply and he clambered into the car, squeezed in beside his brother and sister. Their father started the engine. My hand was waving in front of me. Only Julien and Marie waved back; Max didn't turn around.

I went back to the top of the village and, just before I reached home, since I didn't feel like going inside, I turned right down a path and found myself in the woods. I ran and ran until I couldn't breathe, intoxicated by the smells of late summer, exhilarated, but also feverish at the thought of finding myself alone once more.

37.

School started up again. I did poorly. Everything bored me. Aside from my initial gift for languages and my prodigious memory, I had no talent to speak of. I didn't enjoy writing. I hated doing homework.

Mademoiselle Lavallée and Mademoiselle Fortin had gone; the mayor had been sent an anonymous letter informing him of their loose morals, an accusation backed up by what was said to be irrefutable proof. The two young women were transferred to the other end of the country and never heard of again.

The new schoolmistresses, Mademoiselle Barrault and Mademoiselle Tuque, whom we detested immediately, would separate the boys from the girls each morning and inspect our hands to see if they were clean. Mademoiselle Barrault, who was in charge of the boys, made us line up against the wall then, one by one, we would walk past her, holding our hands out flat. If she deemed a pupil's hands to be insufficiently clean, then the poor boy had to go wash them at the pump outside, with everyone else looking on from their classroom, elbows propped up on the window sills, peering out at him as though he'd committed some heinous crime, and the wrongdoer would then, come what may, have to line up and try again, hoping to pass muster.

I lived in fear of being caught with dirty hands.

38.

I went back to the loft to rummage around in the suit-cases from which my brother had produced the children's clothes. I found the clothing, along with some tiny caps, a few drawings, and stained old photographs of half-naked children, their faces scribbled over with purple ink.

39.

It was thirty degrees in the shade that afternoon. And yet it was already autumn. All we could think of was the heat and our damp bodies. Throughout the village, in every garden hung a heavy, eerie silence, interrupted only by the sound of the stream and the occasional beating of a swallow's wings.

My mother came in from the garden, out of breath, dripping with sweat, her blouse and skirt clinging to her skin. Ducal was right behind her. He entered the kitchen like an excited teenager, skipping and laughing. My mother leaned against the sink and Ducal began to tickle her. She giggled. Like a small animal struggling to cope with the heat, I'd been looking for fresh air, lying on the tiles in a corner of the kitchen. They hadn't seen me. Ducal held my mother's hands as he spoke to her; I didn't catch what he was saying, it wasn't loud enough. Suddenly Ducal put his arms around her and kissed her passionately.

Seeing that upset me so much that I let out a startled cry. That was when France Claudel turned around. She saw me and time stood still for a second or two. She didn't move.

After a pause that seemed to last an eternity, my mother ran a hand through her dishevelled hair and her chapped lips parted as though she was about to say something, but not a sound came from her mouth. She settled on fanning herself with her handkerchief, then turned on her heel and went up to her bedroom.

Ducal was gone in a flash. He disappeared and I didn't see him again that day.

My mother stayed in bed for the rest of the afternoon. My father began to worry when he came home from the bakery to find her still upstairs. He went up to see her. After a long while, he reappeared and told us that our mother was unwell and mustn't be disturbed. He brought her up a bowl of soup that evening and came back down with it right away. "She feels sick," he said, distressed.

We ate without the lady of the house, the four of us, my father having done his best to cook something, and the meal struck me as more upbeat and pleasant than usual.

Maman didn't rise until the following day around noon. A carelessly knotted scarf failed to cover a love bite on her neck. Her hair was unkempt, her eyes were swollen, her lips almost blue, and, without first getting dressed or washing herself, she began to prepare the meal. She called us around one o'clock and we came into the kitchen to see her standing before the fireplace in her bathrobe, her hands outstretched, as though trying to warm herself before the unlit fire.

"Lunch is ready," she said wearily.

She didn't say a word throughout the meal and picked at her plate without really eating. She avoided my gaze. For once she didn't mention my elbows on the table, the noise I made chewing my food, the fork I held in the wrong hand. Putting her to the test, I asked somewhat abruptly, "Maman, would you pass the bread?" She bristled. "Wait until you're offered it." Seemingly out of habit, she added, "Where are your manners? Not so much as a please or thank you!" I gave her a saccharine smile in return, as though daring her to punish me. She stared daggers at me and, at that very moment, a fish bone—it was a Friday—caught in her throat. She pounded the table with her first and began to cough like a witch at the stake. She coughed so hard that she had to go outside into the courtyard. My father followed her nervously and thumped her on the back as though hammering a nail.

40.

I thought my mother would send for me. I was expecting an explanation, a mea culpa, perhaps, or else a phenomenal fit of rage, a punishment. But nothing came. I had witnessed a long, drawn-out kiss between Ducal and my mother. A forbidden kiss. Something would surely come of it.

41.

Autumn days, cold and sad, every one the same as the last. We'd traded in our clogs for rubber boots. All around us the earth was dead, swamped with water; we were vermicelli at the bottom of a bowl of rancid chicken broth, surrounded by pernicious humidity that passed through walls and our clothes.

Max sent me two or three postcards with the Eiffel Tower, the Musée Grévin, or the Jardin des Plantes on one side and, on the other, a short text, full of spelling mistakes, that always began with, "Dear Little Fox" and ended with "Your best friend, Max."

The night before Saint Nicholas was due to arrive, it began to snow. Like every year, I left a glass of water and a carrot in front of the door to our house, as an advance offering to Saint Nicholas for the little gifts, the candies that, I hoped, would be on time and not take two or three days to arrive as with previous years. But by the fifth day there was still nothing, so I asked my mother solemnly:

"Maman, why didn't Saint Nicholas come this year?"

"You probably were too badly behaved. You'll have to wait till next year and try to do better. That'll teach you.

Look out next year or Père Fouettard will come beat you instead."

The glass and the carrot stayed by the door for weeks—a reminder of my wrongdoing, or perhaps her own, and the last of the water that hadn't evaporated began to freeze.

42.

In early January 1954 I was told I would be leaving. They were sending me to a boys' home in Valencourt, a small village fifty kilometres from Mayerville.

It all happened very quickly. My mother packed up my clothes. I was out of the house three days later. I was summoned to the kitchen. My father was standing by the fireplace. The parish priest was there, standing by the window. My mother was leaning against the dresser, arms folded. My father straightened his shoulders and said, as though reciting a text by heart, "You are insufferable, unruly, a dunce, we no longer know what to do with you." I think I saw my mother smile. "We discovered a box buried in the garden. It evidently belongs to you. You should be ashamed of yourself, stealing all those things." They accused me of all kinds of misdeeds, even some I hadn't done, and my father said a curious thing. "I've raised you for eight years. That's enough."

I heard the words "ward of the state," "boys' home," "orphan."

I wondered why I was being sent to live with orphans.

43.

The day before I left, I cried all morning. I didn't want to leave my village. The woods, the fields, the berries, the muddy paths, the Vair, the streams. Having cried my heart out, now mad with rage, I ran to the church square and ripped off all my clothes. I threw them into the fountain and, completely naked, began jumping up and down, waving my arms in the air. Soon I was dancing a mad, demonic dance, shouting gibberish in my tongue and in foreign tongues, the ones I had been given to speak when I was small and that now came back to me. I yelped like an angry little fox and peed everywhere, up against the walls, in the fountain, against the monument to the fallen soldiers, on the carts and motor cars. Mothers shooed their children indoors, covering their eyes, and I went on howling because there was nothing else left to do.

It was the priest who caught me. He wrapped me up in a shawl borrowed from a lady passing by and carried me inside the church, where he set me down beside the statue of the Blessed Virgin. She gave me a smile, I think, as she watched me with a pained but protective expression.

The priest held me in his arms, rocked me like a baby, and, with his thumb, traced a cross on my forehead.

PART III

Who doesn't desire his father's death?

Fyodor Dostoevsky, translated by Constance Garnett,
The Brothers Karamazov

1.

At night, alone in your bed, the moon is your guide, your friend. It protects you... You change into a fox that can be sensed in the darkness but remains unseen. Your only enemies are the wolf and the eagle. You always manage to avoid them, without banishing them from your memories; they continue to harry you.

2.

"What's your name?"
Silence.
"Cat got your tongue?"
Silence.
"Want to come play with us?"
Silence.

3.

I didn't want to get out of the car. They forced me into the building. I sniffled as I gave my name to the warden, wiping my tears away with my sleeve. I lowered my eyes and looked at my feet on the dusty ground.

In the beginning I didn't speak. Me, of all people. In the past there had been no shutting me up, but now I'd lost all powers of speech.

I felt abandoned, like a rotten, worm-ridden plum in some remote orchard.

I didn't eat. In the refectory, I didn't move, my hands resting flat on the table. I stared straight ahead and didn't hear what was being said around me.

I sobbed quietly at night and fell asleep on sheets wet with tears.

4.

Sometimes I heard terrible things about the other boys in the home and their family circumstances. There was talk of young boys who were beaten, mistreated, battered, abused; of babies found in gardens, in dustbins; of brothers who were separated at a young age; of parents who were alcoholics, unemployed, violent, in prison. More often than not, I'd cover my ears. It was best not to hear, best not to know.

5.

One day I told the warden, "I don't understand what I'm doing here. I'm no orphan. My parents aren't dead." He replied, "Not all wards of the state have been orphaned or abandoned. Sometimes parents can no longer look after their children, so the state looks after them instead." I asked the warden if I was to be adopted. No, that was impossible, he said. Only children born to anonymous mothers could be adopted. "And you weren't abandoned," he said. "Well, not exactly." He informed me, as though sharing exciting news, that my mother found me unruly, highly strung, two-faced, impossible to manage. I said, "Yes, I knew that." The warden gave me a dirty look. "Abandoned is the right word," I added. "My parents have abandoned me."

6.

At night, lying on your bed, ever the little fox, you wonder, "If I'm such a good-for-nothing, if I'm so bad, what will become of me? Perhaps I'll be a criminal, a murderer who has police looking for him all over France."

7.

The boys' home comprised a vast building with twenty-three rooms—thirteen on the ground floor (including a refectory), three study rooms, and five classrooms; eight on the first floor and, on the second, two huge dormitories—as well as a courtyard, a urinal, washbasins, a covered playground, a large shed, a wash house, and a thirty-hectare orchard, all surrounded by walls that were two metres in height. The hallways smelled of hard-boiled eggs and the dormitories, of vinegar. There were silverfish by the hundred, crawling along the damp floors by night.

The staff was made up of a warden, two teachers, two supervisors, and a cook; in other words, six adults for seventy children. No cleaning lady, no caretaker. All chores—referred to as "community service"—were carried out by the boys: cleaning, coal, potato, laundry, and gardening duties, on top of six days of classes per week.

Military discipline was required of us from 0630 to 2130 hours. It wasn't quite the nineteenth century, but it was close. It was hard work. My scrawny arms, tiny though they were, soon sprouted little muscles. We always seemed to be holding a scrubbing brush, mop, or bucket. I was often on toilet duty, cleaning up shit and piss. I wanted to throw up the first few times, but I got used to it.

I had an iron bed with a stained mattress in the dormitory on the top floor. It looked down over the garden and, further off in the distance, out over the fields and orchards. The room was dark, even by day. It was stifling hot in summer and freezing cold in winter.

The boys' home was neither a boarding nor a religious school. I didn't return home for the holidays; I was there all year long.

I had very few clothes. We wore shorts practically all year. Aside from shorts, I had a striped suit with starched collar for Sundays and public holidays. My rubber boots had become too small and hurt my feet, so I stayed in clogs through the winter.

We couldn't keep things because everything disappeared. The home was organized a little like a prison. The older boys were in charge and had the final say on everything. They were the ones who passed around clothes, books, merit points, and the holy pictures we got in class. Candies in particular were impossible to hang on to; anything sugary would melt into thin air.

The boys' home was tightly controlled, totalitarian. The teachers were strict, the supervisors ruled with an iron fist, the warden was a despot. Very early on I told myself, "I have to get out of here." The boys, especially the bigger ones who'd been there for a while, the ones who hadn't been adopted, who hadn't been taken back in by their parents, became hardened, embittered, nasty. They took it out on the little ones, made them cry in the hallways, told on them when they'd done something stupid.

At the start, the bigger boys, Jacques, Rufus, Jean-Michel, Big Philippe, would jostle me in the playground, pull my hair, twist my arm. I had no one to complain to: the people who ran the home were on their side. Rufus was particularly cruel. It was said that his father, a communist who had been in the Resistance during the war, had been tortured and decapitated by the Germans. Rumour had it that his head had been sent to his mother as a threat to the family and everyone else in the village. His mother fainted when she opened the box containing the bloodied head, and her head struck a corner of the stove as she fell. They treated her as best they could but, devastated by such cruelty, she simply let herself die. Now orphaned, young Rufus roamed the woods alone for the longest time and he wasn't found until after the war. He was put in the boys' home, never to leave.

Rufus would corner the younger boys in the covered playground and order them to strip. He'd take their clothes and hide them somewhere in the home, leaving the poor kids to make their way back to the dormitory or the refectory naked as the day they were born. Needless to say, general hilarity would ensue. The young boys would often be punished for tomfoolery or for trying to seek attention. The victims wouldn't so much as protest: there was no point.

8.

One day the group of thirteen- and fourteen-year-olds went for a walk in the woods. Big Philippe—we called him Boss—brought back some yellow and gold salamanders. They twisted and turned in a white plastic bucket. One of the boys cut off a salamander's foot to see if it would grow back. I looked down into the bucket and peered halfheartedly at the salamanders. Philippe winked at his friend Jean-Michel. Suddenly Philippe dropped a salamander down my shirt. Surprised, it didn't move at first, then it panicked. I felt it against my skin. It thrashed around, tried to get away, but it was trapped against my lower back, where my skin met the shirt tucked into my shorts. It scurried around to the front, clung to my stomach, and climbed up to my shirt collar. Philippe and his pals sniggered. I wasn't afraid. I didn't cry. I didn't move. When the salamander appeared at my neck, I caught it by the tail, dropped it into my mouth, and began chomping on it as the other boys looked on in astonishment.

9.

Abandoned to the demons of the night, I shed many a tear. I was alone. I would hear the other boys snoring, moaning in their sleep. Often I would hear a voice. It was the G.I. talking to me. His voice, softly accented, soothed and reassured me until I stopped crying. The voice spoke of far-off lands, of an American family that was perhaps also my own, of baseball games, of trips to diners with burgers, milkshakes, and vanilla soda. I'd be lulled by the warm voice, my eyelids growing heavy, my breathing becoming more regular, and I would fall asleep with a smile on my lips, but I'd always wake up in a sweat a few minutes later, often having wet the bed, and I'd call out to the soldier, but he was gone, so I'd cry myself back to sleep.

10.

And then I made some friends: Christian, Gilles, Lulu, Guy, Serge, and Jérôme in particular. We were inseparable. I'd begun to talk again, to have fun again.

Jérôme was an orphan. His parents had died during the war. Of hunger, from the cold, nobody really knew. I didn't dare ask. Jérôme ran everywhere. He was always in a good mood, always ready to play our games, go out on a limb. And yet I could see the distress behind his eyes. I understood that, were he to stop clowning around, to stop running everywhere, he would collapse in a heap and die of a broken heart. Because if anyone's capable of dying of a broken heart, it's a child.

11.

A year after I got there, my mother began visiting me once every two months. She never stayed longer than a half hour. My father never came with her. My sister would come sometimes. She'd make jokes, ask me a ton of questions; she laid it on a bit thick, I think, because she was embarrassed. "Aren't you unhappy?" I'd always just shrug. "Are they treating you well?" My mother would pace around the room, arms folded, looking exhausted, on edge. She'd open the window to smoke while my sister told me what the people of Mayerville were up to. My mother always calmed down after a few cigarettes. She'd sit on the bench by the wall and say, "Come give me a kiss." I'd walk over and press my lips to her powdered cheek. She'd rest her hand on my forehead and on my shoulder. Then, without warning, she'd stand up and leave. My sister would run after her while I remained on the bench, alone, chewing at my fingernails.

12.

I was standing at the end of my bed in my nightshirt.
Time for morning inspection.

A cold shower for those who'd wet the bed.

A cold shower for me.

13.

What I hated more than anything was looking after the pigs. The work was so hard that it would leave me in tears. The other boys made fun of me; they called me a baby, a wimp, a wuss.

14.

I missed Max. The first year, he came to see me at the end of August with his mother. His father waited outside in the car. Madame Bartroz had baked a plum pie. The weather was fine and Max and I played in the yard while Madame Bartroz chatted with the warden under the covered part of the playground. Max asked me all kinds of questions about my life at the boys' home, but I was mostly curious about what he'd been up to all summer in the village, who he'd been playing with. He didn't want to go into detail. He just said with a shrug, "It's not the same without you."

Max didn't know how to say goodbye. He stood there in front of me and began to cry like a little boy. Big, round tears tumbled down onto the dusty ground. I drew closer to him, wanting to hold him in my arms, but the warden rushed over and yanked me back by my shirt collar. Max ran off and got in the car. The sun disappeared all of a sudden, leaving the sky stained with dirty clouds, and it began to rain. Huge drops fell on the dirt, and Madame Bartroz ran to the car, holding up her skirt. As she climbed into the Panhard, she turned to me and waved. Max stared straight ahead. His father started the engine, and I watched the vehicle drive off through the rain. I hurried back to the dormitory, where I flung myself onto my bed and buried my head in my pillow.

15.

December 24. Snow covered the countryside. I found myself with the other children gathered around the Christmas tree in the foyer, a place that was usually gloomy, but that had been decorated for the occasion. We sang Christmas carols and other festive songs. At the foot of the tree, the gifts were so beautifully wrapped that we wondered if they were really for us. I stayed by myself, off in my corner. Jérôme came to get me, tearing me away from my solitude. We were allowed to play all that day. In the refectory, we ate turkey and Brussels sprouts and, for dessert, chocolate gingerbread cake. The warden was wearing a tuxedo (that was too small for him), and the two teachers were dressed the same: each in a black taffeta dress with a fuchsia woolen cardigan. The dresses were much too big and the young women had a hard time walking in their high heels. Their makeup made them look unreal, as though in a movie; we barely recognized them. The two supervisors were dressed in the usual way, only they'd added a tie. The cook was wearing a long, black dress that she no doubt usually wore at funerals. The warden's speech left the staff with tears in their eyes. He thanked everyone and ended on a quote from the Bible.

I was surprised to see no parents there, and on December 25 I waited all day for my mother or sister to visit, but nobody came. Only later did I realize that the whole point of the home was to keep us apart from our families at any cost; family reunions were discouraged, especially over the holidays.

16.

Dragging myself out of bed wasn't easy in winter. The dormitory was freezing cold. I'd open the window, push back the shutters with my scrawny arms, the snow would blind me, I'd close the window again, and rest my head against the glass. I pictured myself running through the snowy woods, crying out in the forest's muted silence.

17.

Often, whenever my thoughts turned to my father, I would have trouble picturing his face. It refused to come into focus. I could summon no more than a sad ghost, as though he were already dead. A silhouette, a shadow, a chimera, a movie image projected against a wall on a summer evening: evanescent, dreamlike, far off in the distance.

18.

Instead of doing my lessons I came up with new languages. I created new countries, new capital cities. I drew maps where previously barren oceans gave birth to invented lands. I imagined myself an explorer, a privateer, a lieutenant, a sailor.

19.

The following summer Max didn't come to see me. He must be ashamed of me, I told myself. He probably didn't understand what I was doing there. Perhaps he was afraid that he, too, would be locked up in that gloomy home for boys. I asked my mother if he'd come to spend the summer with his grandmother like every other year or if he'd stayed in Paris. "I never so much as see the Bartrozes, you know. They're down at the bottom of the village, I don't associate with them." Max's mother came to visit me again. She came with little Marie, who had knitted me a blanket much too small for my bed, but the wool glistened, the stitching was impeccable, it was perfect. At night the blanket shone in the darkness like dying embers and kept me warm. I didn't dare ask Madame Bartroz why Max hadn't come to see me.

20.

The strange sun in the sky. The soft, orange light, the garden behind the house, and the man sitting in his armchair, waiting.

Next to him, on a little table, a book. The title can't be made out: only the word "young" appears, in red letters. Beside the book: a bottle of wine and a glass.

The man, adrift in an immense garden full of tall grasses, scans the horizon. He closes his eyes occasionally. He dozes for a beat then wakes up.

Off in the distance, a woman wearing a flowery dress appears. She turns down the path that leads to the patio at the end of the garden.

She walks slowly, arms outstretched. She's carrying a tray of apples, pears, peaches. The fruits aren't yet ripe: the colours have still to come to life.

The man in the armchair opens an eye. He watches the woman approach. She's pretty in her summer dress. Her body is ravishing; a body that makes you want to reach out and hold her tight, to treasure her. But her face is wan; long wrinkles mark her forehead and she seems nervous, worried. The kind of woman you want to love, but who makes you flee instead. Because she wants everything from life. Life has to be perfect, it's all or nothing with her, and she's always disappointed.

The man, I'm sure of it, is me. And the woman—I'm sure of that, too—is Marie.

21.

Sometimes tyres can be heard crunching on the gravel. Car doors slamming, muffled voices, sobbing in the night. A new boy. We take a good look at him the next morning. He doesn't look at a soul. He cries silently.

22.

The man they called my father didn't come to see me even once. I hated him.

23.

With time I learned to fight and didn't let myself be pushed around. One day I even started a fight with Rufus, shouting at him from across the yard and telling him to pick on someone his own size. Rufus had shoved one of the smaller boys, knocking him to the ground. His knees were bleeding, he was bawling. "Leave him alone!" I shouted. Rufus charged over, grabbed me by the collar, and lifted me off the ground.

"Shut it. Nobody asked you," he said in an authoritative voice that had already broken. "Mind your own business."

He let me go and, without thinking, I spat in his face. He was so shocked he didn't move. I took to my heels and ran off as fast as I could toward the vegetable gardens. He wiped his face on his sleeve and bellowed a war cry, vowing to kill me.

I ran much faster than he did and had time to hide in the shed at the end of the garden, among the tools. I grabbed a shovel and hid beside the door. He drew closer. I waited. As soon as he stepped inside, I thrust the shovel into his face with all my might. The impact was brutal. He fainted. His head was bleeding. They found him hours later. He was moaning. He had to be taken to hospital and we never saw him again. No one ever officially knew who had hit him, but it was rumoured to be me. From that moment on, I was left alone. No one wanted to risk ending up like Rufus, who was said to be disfigured and to suffer from cognitive disorders, including severe memory lapses, that prevented him from identifying his assailant. I had my doubts that a big guy like Rufus was having such a hard time of things. I suspected that he'd quickly recovered from his injuries, barely more than a scratch, and that if he hadn't returned to the boys' home then it was quite simply because he'd been adopted. But I let the rumours do the rounds. They were doing my reputation no harm at all.

24.

One rainy spring, with the help of Jérôme and another friend, Didier, I began a little cigarette-trafficking business. I'd started smoking in secret around the age of eleven and I was never without a pack of Gauloises. I had the cigarettes brought in by one of Didier's cousins, who came to see him every two weeks. The people who ran the home raised their eyebrows at such regular visits, but they didn't say anything. The cousin would bring a big cloth bag full of Gauloises, Gitanes, even lights that we sold for a fortune. Didier would sometimes panic and want to call the whole thing off, but I'd threaten him and he'd keep on going. Jérôme handed the cigarettes out in the yard, in the darker corners of the hallways. It wasn't without risk, as there was always someone keeping an eye on us. I kept track of our sales in a Clairefontaine notebook I hid under my pillow. I didn't really know what I'd spend all the money on, I had no real plan, but week after week it piled up, filling a cake tin I'd buried under a linden tree at the far end of the garden.

25.

One morning I found a dying cat in the yard. Its paw was broken, its tail had been cut off, and it had an open wound above its right eye. I took a large rock and brought it down hard on its head; it died on the spot. In bed that evening I thought of my brother and his little victims, and I sobbed with shame.

26.

Sometimes I would torment the younger boys. I'd swallow earthworms and order them to do the same. They did everything I told them to. I had them eat grass and all kinds of things that took a long time to digest. One day, just to get a reaction, I caught a little grey mouse I'd seen shuffling along the playground wall. I took it by the tail, dropped it gently in my mouth, began to chew, and swallowed it, rubbing my hand on my belly as if my snack couldn't have been more delicious. The boys gathered around me were wide eyed. Some covered their mouths with their hands, trying not to retch.

27.

A cockroach. I glimpsed it in the moonlight. It was scut-
tling along the blanket on the bed next to mine. François
Millet was oblivious. He was fast asleep. The blanket
was pulled up to his chin. The cockroach scurried across
François Millet's lips, along his nose, then over one of
his eyelids. There the disgusting insect paused for a
moment, wriggling its long, fine antennae. It seemed
to be thinking. "What shall I do? Where shall I go?" It
began turning in circles. Suddenly it tried to get inside
his eye. Having met with no success, it circled around
again, then continued on its way, crawling over the
forehead of François Millet, who was snoring softly, and
disappearing into the hair of our sleeping roommate.

28.

Sometimes they made us write to our parents (those of us who had any). I sent a postcard from the boys' home. I didn't know what to say, so I scribbled:

From the boys' home with love.

29.

Once a month we had movie night. They'd show us scratchy old copies of mostly out-of-date films: *Les Disparus de Saint-Agil*, *Fanfan la Tulipe*, *Ignace*, and others whose titles I've forgotten.

30.

Jérôme was behaving very strangely. He wouldn't look me in the eye. He'd become distant. I asked around and found out he was keeping a share of the money for himself. He was selling the cigarettes for much more than we'd agreed on and pocketing the profits. One day Jérôme was questioned by the warden, who was surprised at the number of cigarettes in circulation in the home, and the game was up. Jérôme also told him where I'd buried the cake tin containing my spoils. They really let me have it. The strap, no food, no going outside, chores day and night.

31.

I was angry. I didn't want to see another soul. I stayed in bed all day. They tried to drag me out, but I clung to the bars and screamed. I emptied my head of all thoughts; my entire body given over to rage. It was as though I was no longer human, nothing but a ball of flesh and blood, hurt and wounded. But then one day I reappeared in the refectory and sat down at my usual place as though all was right in the world. The others looked at me; there was sadness, but also fear, in their eyes. I'd had enough of my prison.

32.

Once a week we'd go for a walk around the village, two
boys to a row, led by one of the supervisors. We would
go to the grocery store that doubled as a bar and tobacconist's. The children who had a few centimes on them
would buy sweets and candy bars, Coco Boers, and
sticks of licorice; the richer ones, postcards or figurines.
I'd get bored in the store—when it came down to it, they
didn't have very much and, at any rate, I didn't have any
money. My box had been discovered and all the profits from my cigarette racket had been confiscated. As
soon as the sales clerk turned his back, I'd hide a few
goodies up my shirt. On our way back, we'd pass by the
church. I liked it there. I preferred it to the chapel at
the boys' home, a former classroom that, in spite of the
Christian knickknacks, in no way resembled a place of
worship. Inside the church were lots of wooden sculp-
tures, tobacco-coloured curtains, two angels painted
above the stained glass, an altar, a superb sculpture of
Christ, completely naked, a blue Virgin Mary with a
milky white face, that I adored, but at the foot of which
I could not kneel, unfortunately, as I would have done

before the Black Madonna in Mayerville, since I was never alone and we were always pressed for time. We were always in a hurry back. I would wonder why, since time stood still at the boys' home, each long, agonizing day much like the one before it, and the next to come. Why the rush? The supervisors no doubt lived in fear of one of us running off. They would look around in every direction, panic-stricken. If one of us were to escape, there would be hell to pay. The people who ran the home were unforgiving.

33.

It was on one of those walks that I ran away. I simply dropped the hand of the boy standing beside me and that was that. He looked at me stupidly, in utter amazement. I ran as fast as I could, heading for the fields, the orchards. The supervisor cried, "Émile, come back!" He hesitated before chasing after me. I ran and ran, terrorized and drunk with freedom. The poor man didn't run for very long. He stopped, out of breath, hands on knees. "Don't do this!" he shouted. And I ran even harder.

34.

Whole days spent walking, waiting, suffering.

35.

I passed through sleepy, morose villages with mysterious names: Coussey, Autigny-la-Tour, Soulosse-sous-Saint-Élophe, Liffol-le-Grand. I wound my way along dusty paths, cut across meadows, and ate wild berries and mushrooms. Whenever I saw farmers on their tractors, out in the fields with their ploughs, I hid. My toes were bleeding, my knees were scraped raw. The little cuts took ages to heal because I would always rip the scabs off. I bathed in the Vair and dried off in the sun. I slept at the foot of trees, curled up in their roots. I'd wake in the morning, my eyelashes stuck together, a bitter taste in my mouth, my hair covered with leaves, twigs, and mud.

36.

One day I noticed a big, black hole halfway up a hill. A voice summoned me inside and, although charmed by the gentle murmur that called out to me, I was terrorized by the cavernous hole. I gathered my courage and went inside the cave. There was a smaller opening at the back, just wide enough to let my body pass. Concealed within the rock face, my hiding place was perfect.

I made myself a makeshift bed of straw and dead leaves. At night I heard the bats flying above me and the water burbling behind the rock. I thought of Max. I imagined him in Paris in a little three-piece suit, strolling down the Champs-Élysées, in the Jardin des Plantes, at the Eiffel Tower. I could picture the Bartroz family in their apartment in the eighteenth arrondissement, little Marie in a white dress sitting at the dining-room table with its red gingham tablecloth, drawing or perhaps knitting. Madame Bartroz was carrying in sophisticated dishes of food. Sitting in a leather armchair, Monsieur Bartroz was smoking his pipe and reading the newspaper. Did they ever think of me? Did they ever try to imagine, when night fell, what I was going through?

Some nights I would shiver with cold. I would hear the water flowing in the Vair, the rustling leaves of the beech and spruce trees, the owls hooting. There were rats all around me. I couldn't see them, but I could sense them.

One day I came across a cabin in the woods. It was full of all kinds of things, including an old frying pan, matches, and moth-eaten blankets. I took it all with me and, early the next morning, I set off fishing and, that evening, lit a fire in the cave and cooked a meal fit for a king. I fell asleep with a full belly.

When I walked along the Vair or through the meadows, I would sometimes hear people out for a walk and I'd run as far away from them as I could.

My red hair was getting long. I tied it back in a ponytail with a piece of twine I'd found in the cabin.

One day I was walking behind the houses looking for vegetables in the gardens when I saw a little girl run out of a house. She stopped in her tracks when she saw me standing among the leeks. I pressed my index finger to my lips and went, "Sssh." She stayed stock-still, watching me as she sucked her thumb. I pulled up leeks and unearthed potatoes and carrots, carrying them away in a basket of sorts I made by turning up the bottom of my shirt.

I went back to the same garden the next day and the little girl was having a tea party on the grass. She chatted to her dolls and scolded them because they weren't hungry. She jumped when she realized I was there. I didn't

222

move. Squatting between two rows of strawberries, I stuffed the fruit into my mouth. The little girl stood up and came over to me. She handed me a piece of bread, which I took with a smile. Someone called her from inside the house and she turned around. I ran away.

Every day after that, as soon as I arrived, she brought me all kinds of food that she'd kept for me. She gave me a little basket that I brought back each time I visited. She would fill it with chunks of dried sausage, crackers, hardened bits of meat, and sometimes even one or two little cakes that I would gobble down there and then.

One day the girl stopped coming. At first I thought that she and her parents had moved house or had gone on a family holiday. But I was wrong. One morning I spied the little girl watching me from the window. Her little scheme had no doubt been uncovered and she wasn't allowed out anymore. I motioned for her to come down, but she took a step back and disappeared into the darkness of the room and I never saw her again.

In another village, one day an old woman found me in her vegetable garden. Instead of sending me packing, she invited me into her kitchen. "Don't be frightened," she said. "Come in!" I really wasn't sure, but I was intrigued and walked over to her, slowly, my steps hesitant. The old woman stepped back into the room, holding bread and cheese in one hand, and I stepped forward. I kneeled down in front of her stove; she ran a hand through my hair and passed me the food. I devoured the lot. Then, having eaten my fill, I stood up and ran away.

The following day the old woman saw me coming down the path behind her garden and called out to me. I hesitated, but she was very patient. As I reached the kitchen door, she pointed to a chair and motioned for me to sit down. I went over to the table and took a seat. She took three eggs, which she broke into a bowl, and added a little milk. She mixed it all together and made me an omelette. She was humming a tune I didn't know, a lullaby I'd never heard, something about a donkey skin.

I came back every day, until the old lady decided to keep me. One morning she locked the door behind me. The key turned twice in the lock and, gripped by panic, I knocked over the table and chairs, begging her to let me go. She said, "I'll take good care of you. You'll live here with me." I shook my head and pulled at the door handle. In tears, I ran up the stairs. She didn't have time to catch me. I opened her bedroom window and jumped down into the garden. It was a big drop, but my body was supple. I ran off without looking back.

Road Kill

Angry little animal
Gathers speed recklessly
But surprised by the lights of a car
Freezes, transfixed.
And is soon lying on the ground
In an unfortunate mess.

38.

He was a very tall man, in his early twenties, red hair, silver sideburns, milky white skin with a smattering of spots on his forehead, a long nose, straight and fine, charming little eyes with very black pupils, a perfect mouth, sensual and symmetrical. He held a helmet under his arm, he was a G.I. It was him, the American soldier. He was smiling. Two dimples in his cheeks. He was standing before me, waiting. He began to speak very softly. He said, "How are you? You're not lonely?" I held out a piece of fish and a cob of corn I'd grilled the night before. He came toward me, took the food, and grimaced as he kneeled down.

ÉMILE
Does it hurt?
JACK
My injury still bothers me. I have cramps, rheumatism. Sometimes I walk with a limp.
A long silence.
ÉMILE
Do you love your wife? Your children?

JACK

Of course, what questions! Who doesn't love their children?

ÉMILE

I know parents who don't love their children.

JACK

Don't be silly.

ÉMILE

Did you love my mother?

JACK

France? You don't ask questions like that.

ÉMILE

But I'm interested.

JACK

Love's complicated, you know. I love my wife.

ÉMILE

But you weren't married during the war. Did you love my mother?

JACK

Times were hard during the war. All kinds of relationships are struck up during conflicts, some of them very bizarre. But they seldom last.

ÉMILE

Did you know Ducal?

JACK

Yes, of course. We kept a close eye on him while we were there. He was suspected of collaborating with the Germans.

ÉMILE

Was he?

JACK

Probably.

ÉMILE

Was he in love with my mother?

JACK

Ducal? He's an old man! He's much older than your mother, isn't he?

ÉMILE

He's not that old.

JACK

Personally, I thought he had skin like a leaf in fall, his breath was foul, and he had the grey eyes of a dead man.

ÉMILE

Do you think we look like each other?

JACK

Who? You and Ducal?

ÉMILE

No, you and me.

JACK

You and me? No, not at all. No, I don't think so. Why do you ask?

39.

Émile, you're a little boy who cries often, all alone, your head buried in your arms, you dream that you burrow into your bed like an animal burrows into the ground, you imagine you're ill, like that bedridden young cowboy with everyone gathered around him in that western you saw at the cinema a long time ago, everyone promising him he'd get better and him moaning with pain or was it pleasure? Émile, you are a little boy who isn't like a fox, who isn't cunning, deep inside you have a love that you don't know how to express, but that love is real. You often worry, because once you have children you don't know how you'll show your love. The thought of it torments you and brings you to tears, because you're afraid you won't be up to the job.

40

Our Lady of the Daisies

I went to the woods
And there I found a church
A simple church, flanked by daisies.
Out came a pretty woman who shook
A handkerchief and who, from afar,
Calmly began blowing me kisses.

41.

JACK

Why are you crying, little Émile?

ÉMILE

It's nothing...

JACK

Your mother wrote me. She says she's been very worried since you disappeared from boarding school.

ÉMILE

It wasn't boarding school. I never went home. I was in prison.

JACK

Don't be so dramatic. Your mother went to see you, didn't she?

ÉMILE

No, not once!

JACK

Don't cry. Relax. I'll tell you a story.

42.

One morning I spied a little hare come out of its hole, look right, left, hesitate, it saw me and was about to go back into its burrow, but it changed its mind and hopped merrily over to the meadow, passing in front of me as if I wasn't there.

43.

A dream. A magician, tall and handsome, black hair slicked back. With a wave of his magic wand, a flick of his cape, elegance in motion, he produces a pure white rabbit from his hat, and then waves his wand again. The audience expects something else to emerge from the top hat, but it's always the same rabbit, so very white, so surprised to be there, and the children applaud silently, and they laugh their heads off, and the rabbit comes out of the hat again, and the magician, always with the same, expert hand, with a wave of his magic wand, a flick of the cape, produces a rabbit from his hat, so very white, so surprised to be there.

44.

A fox, unable to reach the grapes that were growing high on the vine, reasoned they weren't ripe, that he didn't want them anyway. — Charles Perrault, "The Fox and the Grapes"

45.

Sooner or later you'll wake up.

46.

One morning I decided to go into Neufchâteau. I'd been chased out of all the vegetable gardens and had nothing left to eat. I planned to go around the markets, steal from the shops, or rummage around in a few bins.

I made my way through thick fog, striding out across wet fields, taking detour after detour, before reaching the main road. I passed through Ban-de-Maxey. I'd often heard of the village, but had never been. People said that, one Sunday after the war, a nine-year-old boy who was tending sheep had seen the Blessed Virgin and that she had spoken to him. There must have been something in the air: the village wasn't far from Domrémy-la-Pucelle. The little boy had seen a pale glow, then a blinding light, with a beautiful woman standing in the middle of it. She was smiling and held out an arm as though wanting to touch the boy. Joseph Bailly—that was the boy's name—was so stunned he stood rooted to the ground, his mouth hanging open, his hand to his chest. He listened to what the beautiful woman was saying and he began to cry. Later he told the parish priest and others who questioned him that the beautiful woman's voice was absolutely magnificent, as pure as any musical instrument, and that, in her every word, he had felt all the sadness of the mysterious lady as she spoke of all the children who had died in the war and of the impiety of Christians. She tasked little Joseph with making those things known to his people. Moreover, the Blessed Virgin had shared a personal secret with him, a secret that never was revealed.

Joseph Bailly's tale struck a chord, and the story spread quickly across the region. The bishop of Nancy set up a commission to investigate the event and, unfortunately for young Bailly, the commission concluded that he had been lying. A little girl told her mother that Joseph had invented the whole thing so as to draw attention to himself. When Bailly was questioned further, he backed down and admitted he'd made it all up. No one really knew what happened to the little boy after that. There was talk of an unhappy, meandering life; he was rumoured to have drowned in the Vair, gobbled up by hungry pike.

In Neufchâteau, I wandered the streets that were nearly deserted at that hour of the morning. A market was setting up in a square. I worked up the courage to approach a few of the stallholders, my eyes imploring, and was handed an apple and a hunk of cervelas sausage. As soon as the questions began—"What are you doing here?" "Where are you from?" "How old are you?"—I ran off. I walked around the church and onto the main street, looking at the window displays, a baker's, a butcher's, a jeweler's. On that bleak morning, the grey buildings seemed tall and menacing. Some passersby cast me sidelong glances, an unspoken, almost hostile question in their eyes: "Who is this filthy boy, this scruffy urchin?"

I begged at the station and was tossed a few francs. I went into a dimly lit café, sat at the back where no one could see me. I ordered a hot chocolate and a croissant. The waiter gave me a dirty look. He brought over the order and made me pay right away. I took the coins out of my pocket and rolled them across the table. A woman sitting by the window gave me a long, hard stare. She stood up and came over.

"Goodness, you're so thin," she said. "Where are you from? I haven't seen you around."

I shrugged.

"Don't feel like answering? I don't bite, you know."

"I'm not from around here," I said, getting up, ready to leave.

"No, don't go," she pleaded, pushing me back down onto my chair with a gentle but firm hand. "Stay here. I'll get you something. What are you drinking?"

"Hot chocolate."

She called over the waiter. She ordered another hot chocolate and asked him for a basket of croissants.

I ate them up in a flash. I downed my drink without waiting for it to cool, and burned my tongue. My Good Samaritan looked at me the way you'd look at a little animal. She smiled. I didn't want to become attached and I didn't want her to get attached to me either, so I stood up and ran outside. "Wait," she cried. I ran as fast as I could, without looking back. I turned right and went down a side street.

A man was sitting on a stone bench, leaning forward, elbows on his knees, sweat streaming down his face. I was tempted to make an about-turn, but it was too late, I'd gone too far. I passed him as quickly as I could, but he called out to me and grabbed at my sleeve. "Who are you, boy? What are you doing lurking around here?" He stood and cracked his knuckles. I walked a little quicker and looked back after a minute. He was still behind me, hands in his pockets, a Gitane hanging from his lips. He called out gently, "Come back, kid. Don't be scared. I don't want to hurt you." I think he called me by my name. How did he know me? I'd never seen him before. I walked faster and faster, but he stayed close. I turned down a dark alley and that was where he caught up to me and was suddenly standing in front of me, his cigarette still dangling from his lips.

He gave me a strange smile. His hair was jet black, he had long eyelashes; he looked like he was wearing makeup. He was young, but he looked a little like Old Ducal. He might have been his son, but Ducal didn't have any children.

"What are you so scared of?" he asked, affectedly.

I said the first thing that came into my head:

"My father's waiting for me at the end of the street. He'll be worried. Let me go."

239

He began to laugh. His teeth were all rotten and his breath stank of alcohol.

"I just want to touch you," he said in a deep voice.

I winced in disgust.

He reached out with his hand and stroked my cheek. Then he put two fingers inside my mouth. I was very afraid. Suddenly someone turned into the alley. I gave the young man a shove and managed to get away. I ran without looking back, as hard as I could, my lungs and stomach bursting with air, and I headed back in the direction of the courthouse, hurrying through the deserted streets. I came to a stop beneath a carriage entrance, out of breath, bent double, heart hammering. A dog barked. I heard footsteps, a voice calling out, and I was off again, not stopping until I reached the edge of town. I went back to my forest, my cave, and I lay down on my makeshift bed and fell into the deepest of sleeps.

47.

I awoke in the middle of the night. I saw the G.I. come into the cave. He kneeled down beside my bed. "Émile, you'll never learn," he said. "You're nothing but a filthy animal." He reached out with his hands, began to strangle me, and my face turned red. I couldn't breathe. There was a mix of fear and surprise in my eyes. And suddenly he let go, and that was when I woke up, shouting. I looked around me. A little candle flickered in the darkness; shadows dancing along the walls; and, aside from my ragged breathing, the silence was perfect.

48.

A few weeks later, I returned to Neufchâteau. The town drew me to it. I felt alone and needed to see shoppers walking down the busy streets. I was also hungry and thirsty, and I needed a new frying pan and a blanket (I missed Marie's terribly). I skirted around the neighbourhood where the man had followed me and, in a part of town I didn't know, I came across a carnival. It didn't take long to realize it was the same troupe I'd seen in Mayerville before moving to the boys' home. I glimpsed the tent belonging to Marmol the Magician in the distance and approached it discreetly. I saw him working at something outside his caravan. I watched him come and go. He and his assistant Dimitri, alias Pim, were getting ready for that night's show.

Suddenly Marmol was behind me, yanking me by the collar.

"What are you doing here? Why are you spying on me?"

"I'm not spying on you," I said, turning my head.

"Why, I know you... That red hair of yours, that long face, that pointy snout, those little toast-coloured paws.

You're the little rascal who tried to steal the show on my stage in that godforsaken village. What was it called? Masserville? Martinville?"

"Mayerville," I said.

I wanted to pipe up that I wasn't a "rascal," I wasn't the "animal" he was describing. "What gives you the right?" I wanted to demand, but he went on.

"Just look at yourself! Look at the state of you! You're filthy. You stink."

I shrugged and went to leave, but then he said a strange thing that made me turn back.

"I know where you're hiding in the forest," he murmured.

Since I didn't reply, he went on:

"I know you ran away and now you're living in a cave."

I eyed him suspiciously, then ran as far away from him as I could.

The next day, I was back hanging around the square. Pim was sitting on a chair outside the magician's caravan. He waved me closer, and I approached shyly.

"Marmol said you were sniffing around. Are you alone? You're not with your parents?"

"They're dead."

"What? You're pulling my leg."

"No, not at all. They died in a road accident."

He eyed me up and down, a smile on his lips. He lit a cigarette and, before putting the pack away, passed it to me. I took one.

We smoked in silence. Suddenly he said:

"Would you like to see the magician's show?"

"I already have, and I have no money."

"He has new acts now. It's much more sophisticated than it used to be, believe me. I can get you in without paying, if you like."

I still wasn't sure, but I said:

"Okay then."

"Come back later," said Pim, giving me a broad smile. "Meet me backstage."

When I got there, Pim was dressed for the performance, made-up and freshly shaved, smoking a cigarette. "I didn't think you'd come," he said. He tossed his cigarette butt on the ground and showed me in through the side of the tent. The show was about to start, and the lights dimmed. In the darkness, I headed straight for an empty seat in the third row. I felt uncomfortable, no longer used to being around so many people. The show was virtually identical to the one I'd seen in Mayerville. Pim had been lying: there were no new acts.

Marmol was sweating heavily, and bungled his act more than once.

After the levitation number featuring the young girl disappearing into thin air, Marmol came down from the stage and headed straight for me. I kept my head down, thinking he'd keep going right to the back of the tent, but he stopped in front of me, arms folded. "Well, well, dear friend. Please come join me. I know you want to, I can tell." My cheeks on fire, I looked right then left. All eyes were on me. There was no getting away. I stood up shyly. Grabbing me swiftly by the arm, Marmol dragged me up onto the stage, where a full-length mirror had just been set down by Pim. Marmol performed a variation of the routine I'd seen in Mayerville. He had me stand in front of the mirror. I waited there patiently, my back to the audience. The magician brandished his magic wand, pronounced the magic words in Latin, and, instead of my reflection in the mirror, there appeared a series of figures, each more outlandish than the last. First there was a girl, who bore a disturbing resemblance to little Marie; then a great white, bespectacled rabbit, just like in *Alice in Wonderland*, which made the children laugh; then an old hunchbacked lady wearing a housedress and a headscarf; and, finally, a fine-looking fox with red fur but a threatening look in its eyes, a sight that caused me great sorrow. I began to cry. The magician saw my tears and the fox's reflection disappeared as quickly as it had appeared, replaced by that of my ten-year-old body. Applause, a little bow to the audience, a handkerchief held out by Pim with which to dry my eyes, and the magician motioned for me to sit back down.

After the show, Pim came to ask me to join him backstage. He had me sit on a chair and I waited, hands on knees. Pim stood beside me; he was waiting, too.

Marmol burst into the room without warning. He was still wearing his magician's outfit, but he spoke normally, without the histrionics he employed on stage. My heart was beating hard. What did he want from me?

"I need a helping hand," he said.

I looked at him, wide-eyed.

"I need an assistant... someone to help with the housework, the ironing, the washing... as well as the odd magic trick, new routines I hope to perform next year."

"Say yes," Pim said, elbowing me.

I didn't really know what to say, so I just said, "Yes."

49.

Two days later I left with the rest of the troupe. I sat next to Marmol in the motorcar hitched to his old caravan. The whole way, the conjurer told one story after the other, each as implausible as the last, trying to impress me. He told me about the time he met Houdini. "I met Houdini in the flesh in 1913. He'd come to Europe after a triumphant tour across the United States. I was still a teenager. There was a new addition to his show—the most extraordinary escape of his career, The Water Torture Cell. After the show, he met a few carefully selected fans. I panicked when my turn came to shake his hand; I almost fainted. He realized I was shy and not feeling very well, so he put a hand on my shoulder—my heart rate slowed instantly—and took me in his arms. A sensation of absolute calm washed over me, and my mind cleared completely. He stepped back, looked me in the eye, and said, 'You'll be a magician, my friend.'"

We drove through Lorraine, Champagne-Ardenne, even Luxembourg and Belgium. I learned that Marmol wasn't French but Belgian, and that his grandfather was Irish. We all slept in the caravan. The magician used to dry his underwear on a clothesline that he strung up from the kitchen light to the top of a cupboard; his huge underpants were stained and his undershirts were grey rather than white. There were no latrines, so we used public toilets or simply went in the woods. The magician had an enormous appetite, and I could see him putting on weight by the day. He drank, too. A lot.

I would have long conversations with the tightrope walker who was part of the troupe. Like all tightrope walkers, he came from a family of them. He would often stretch his rope from the village church to the roof of the town hall. He smoked a lot, which made him cough, so sometimes he'd lose his balance and a nervous murmur would ripple through the crowd, but he never fell; he was too sure-footed for that.

The woman with no limbs hadn't always been without limbs. She told me she lost her arms and legs in a car accident. She was often foul-tempered and was still struggling to come to terms with her handicap: before her accident, she'd enjoyed running and spending time in the forest. "I feel like a prisoner," she'd say, sadly. She couldn't bear how the audience stared, the inappropriate comments made by children or by teenagers who'd been drinking. When I visited her in her caravan, I'd make us tea and she'd tell me about her life before. She said, "Did you know I had three babies and they all died?" Or "Did you know my husband left me after the accident because he couldn't stomach the sight of my stumps?"

I'd visit Sylvie, an enormous red-haired woman who would put her nearly naked body on display for all to see in one of the circus tents, to the public's great delight and consternation. She might have been fat and flabby, with a goiter and two huge misshapen breasts that rolled around under her camisole down near her waist, but I thought she was gorgeous. She lived alone in her caravan and had a hard time walking. I visited her every day. She'd give me candy and tell me fairy tales. "Do you know the story of Donkeyskin's son?" I shrugged. "I know the fable about Donkeyskin," I said, "but not about her son." She clapped her hands and exclaimed, "Excellent! Let me tell you it then."

50.

Not long after she was married, Donkeyskin had a son. The child had clear, almost transparent, skin; his eyes were deep and honest; his hair, of silk; his build, fragile. Admired, envied, venerated, the queen's son was the most popular boy in the kingdom. Girls snatched up the figurines of him that were sold by travelling salesmen. Boys were jealous and called him a girl behind his back, finding him too pompous, too sophisticated, to one day be king. He was remarkably intelligent and, by the age of eight, he'd already read every novel, tried every trade, visited every country. His mother cared for him as though tending to a sick child. He took up all her attention, every day of every year, and his every wish was granted.

The son knew his mother's story. He had been struck by the tragic tale of the grandfather who wanted to marry his daughter, heartened that she had been able to run off and hide in order to escape infamy, and impressed by the prince's gallant determination to track her down. But the son also knew that his mother quickly became disenchanted after her wedding. Her husband was always off hunting, seldom seen at court. Even when he wasn't hunting, he would leave the castle at dawn, saddling his horse himself and venturing deep into the lowlands. He was a solitary soul, an anxious man who did not enjoy the company of women and, indeed, feared them.

Donkeyskin was left in charge, but even though her days were full, she grew bored. Languishing in her melancholic castle surrounded by swampland, she began drinking and, by afternoon, would be in a trance-like state, stretched out on a chaise longue, half asleep. She took on lovers, some of whom attempted to distance her from her son. This would sometimes fill her with indignation, but often she put up no resistance and her son would withdraw to his room, sobbing quietly. He would muffle his cries of despair in his pillow and murmur in a crystal-clear voice, "I wish I would fall asleep and never wake up." His mother, once so present, was now painfully absent.

One day his mother, who had been drinking heavily, staggered into her son's room, shouting that she loved him. Her lover had just left her, she was hiccupping, and great big tears were rolling down her cheeks. "I love you so much," she told her son as she stepped toward him. "My son, my little wonder, I love you so." The son didn't know what to think. His mother had become unrecognizable. She hadn't changed her clothes in two days. She had large sweat stains around her armpits, her platinum blonde hair was straggly and sorely in need of a comb, and her makeup was running. His mother drew ever closer. The son propped himself up on an elbow. He was frightened and at once ashamed. What child is frightened of its own mother?

Donkeyskin sat on her son's bed. She stroked his cheek, then his hair. In her drunken state, Donkeyskin's touch was clumsy, awkward. She took her son in her arms and began to snivel. "Oh, I'm so unhappy," she said. "You're all I have." The son was embarrassed. Her loving—almost brutal—embrace was totally inappropriate.

After a time, Donkeyskin released her son, then she clasped his head in her hands and kissed him on the lips. Once, then twice. The third time, the son was sure she was probing around for his tongue. He turned his head away, appalled, disgusted by the woman he had once loved, who he had once worshipped. "*You*'re faithful to me," his mother said as she stroked his cheek. "*You* really love me." She held him tight and tried to kiss him again, but the son pulled away, crying "No, no, no!" and leapt to his feet. He looked frail and vulnerable in his colourful pyjamas. In a panic, he ran to the door and out into the castle hallways. He could hear his mother shouting, "Come back, my child. Please forgive me," still in the throes of delirium, but he covered his ears. He didn't want to hear another word from that madwoman.

Shocked at his family history repeating itself, terrorized by the idea that his mother would surely wish to marry him should her husband die, the son decided to flee the castle. He ran through the forest for days at a time, his mother's words still ringing in his ears. And yet she was already far, far away, and every day a little further still.

After a week, the son came across a cowshed and stopped to catch his breath. He struggled to find the strength to continue, but fell asleep. The mooing of a cow roused him. For a moment he didn't know where he was, then he came to his senses. He looked around and saw a little workshop and some tools. He picked up a long knife, still in its sheath, and stuffed it in his belt.

The son set off again and came face to face with a bear. He fought it bravely. He didn't know his own strength, but he managed to strangle the animal bare-handed, and it soon lay dying in the undergrowth. He cut it up and took its pelt, which he dried and put on his back so as to disguise himself. Unfortunately, as the son passed through the villages, people recognized him at once. Everyone knew his mother's story and they immediately made the leap from a donkey disguise for the mother to a bear disguise for the son. "What a story, all the same!" they said. And, "Do people never learn?"

A fairy by the name of Morgan, a legendary creature that people in the region called a "mago," landed on the shoulder of the son as he was crossing a river, the bear pelt on his back. Morgan whispered in his ear, advising him to get rid of the bear pelt since his mother would have little trouble finding him in his none-too-subtle disguise. The mago told him he should dress as a girl instead. "But how?" the son asked. "I'll take care of it," the mago said, disappearing in a puff of smoke.

The son continued on his way and passed through a village. People stared at him and laughed. Children ran circles around him and began to push and shove him.

On his way out of the village, the son stopped at a spring. He gulped down the fresh water and washed his face. Suddenly there was a rustling in the bushes and Morgan appeared. He shone as though there was a light inside him, and he settled on the hand of the son. "Go behind that bush," the mago said, "and you'll find something to change into." The son hesitated for a moment, then he went into the bushes and found a small pile of clothes. The mago flew after him and said, "Here you go, my friend. Get changed. Here's a dress, a wig, some makeup." The son took off the bear pelt, freeing himself at last from the weight of the risible disguise and its foul smell. He felt lighter at once. He took the girl's clothes and got dressed. The mago applied the lipstick, eyeshadow, and rouge, and said, "No one'll be any the wiser!"

The son made a very pretty girl. A delicate child, with fine features and no shortage of grace.

He passed through other villages, moving further and further away from the castle, from his mother.

One day he stopped by the side of the road and overheard two gleaners talking. The son learned that the king, his father, had fallen from his horse in a tournament and died. The son cried for his father even though, when all was said and done, he hadn't spent much time with him. The son was seized by panic, since, with his father dead, people would be looking for him everywhere. His mother would be wanting one thing and one thing only: to marry her son. History would repeat itself. And so the son distanced himself even further from the region where he was born and ventured into unknown lands where no one spoke his language.

One July afternoon he spotted a girl dressed in rags sitting cross-legged on the steps of a church, her face worn by the wind and the sun, scabs on her knees, and, in spite of it all, he found her strikingly beautiful. He tried to avoid her, but she called out to him, "Come over here!"

He approached.

"You speak my tongue?" the son asked.

"Of course I do!"

"I didn't think anyone did here."

She shrugged and asked:

"What's your name?"

"I don't have a name."

"What do you mean, you don't have a name? Everyone has a name."

"I'd rather not say."

"Why not?"

"It's a secret."

"Are people looking for you? Are you on the run, is that it? Did you steal something?"

The son didn't reply, and the young girl stood, took him by the hand, and led him to a house at the end of the village. The son saw no boys along the way. Only girls lived there. Young girls with long, braided hair, long linen dresses, and padded leather sandals, girls who held each other by the hand and laughed heartily. "This is where I live," said the young girl who'd been sitting on the church steps. "Make yourself at home. You can stay as long as you'd like." The son slept for days. Stretched out on a crude but comfortable bed, he dreamed of his mother. She was standing on a chair in the middle of a room, drunk as could be, shouting that she was calling off the search for her son. "I no longer have a son," she shouted. "He's gone forever." In his dream, the mother wobbled and toppled backward off the chair. Her head struck the stone floor and blood trickled into the cracks between the tiles.

His new companion was called Belladine. One day she came and lay down beside the son and caressed him for hours. They made love, gently touching each other with the tips of their fingers. They loved each other day and night. Belladine loaned him clothes, and it was as a girl that Donkeyskin's son went on living his life.

51.

Marmol was a terrible magician. Breaking into a sweat, he would sometimes be overcome with dizziness and drop his cards and scarves. One day he became unwell in the middle of his act and had to be taken backstage. He pressed his hand to his heart, as though it might stop. The crowd was asked to be patient. People looked at each other without really understanding what was going on. Marmol came back out thirty minutes later. He had changed costumes and looked much younger. His makeup was fresh and he picked up where he'd left off. But he soon bungled his routine again, and people began to leave.

52.

Marmol taught me magic tricks. Cards, glasses, and coins. He came up with the idea of using me during his act, having me tumble around, tie my body in knots. I walked on my hands, contorted my body every which way. I did the splits, I squeezed my whole body into see-through boxes that were much too small. I practiced in the caravan in the evenings and, soon enough, I was able to fit into smaller and smaller boxes—to the audience's great astonishment.

53.

I often missed the forest and would run off at night. Marmol was a sound sleeper and Pim snored loudly. I'd slip outside soundlessly and run flat out.

Marmol came up to me one morning and put a hand on my shoulder.

"What were you doing outside last night?" he asked.

I frowned and pretended not to understand.

Since I didn't reply, he said:

"I don't want you going out at night."

"Why not?"

"Because I'm in charge here. What were you doing out so late?"

"Nothing."

"I want to know what you're up to. Are you stealing? Is that it?"

"No, nothing like that. I go running in the woods. I watch the animals."

I walked into the kitchen and gathered the ingredients for breakfast.

He followed and stood just behind me.

"I don't want you getting hurt," he murmured in my ear. "It could get in the way of your contortion routine, got it? I'm here to keep an eye on you. I'm here to guide you. You're to do what I say."

I broke five eggs into a bowl and whipped them with a fork, adding salt and pepper. Marmol started to talk some more.

"You think I'm an idiot. You think I don't see what's going on. But I know you're up to something."

I'd had enough of his accusations. I sighed theatrically.

"Sometimes I can't sleep," I said. "So I go running in the woods. Is that a crime?"

I regretted my words as soon as I said them. No doubt he would make me pay for my insolence.

"You cheeky little... That's not what I'm talking about. Don't act all innocent. I know you're stealing money from me."

I grabbed a frying pan, threw some butter into it, and lit the gas. I took my time, then I turned around.

"Money?"

"Yes, money, and more as well. Just wait till I find where you're hiding it."

Since I didn't answer, he leaned in and struck the back of my neck with his big, clammy hand. Then he stepped back and went outside.

I heard Pim getting up. He walked into the kitchen, naked as the day he was born, scratching his testicles. His penis was enormous, half erect.

"What's for breakfast?" he asked.

"You'll see," I said, turning back.

54.

Marmol and Pim would play cards in the evenings. I never wanted to. I preferred reading in a corner of the caravan. One night they made me. "No, I'm not interested," I said. His eyes angry, Pim shouted, "Get over here and sit down!" Pim stood and rushed at me. He grabbed my ear like I was a little boy who'd been misbehaving and dragged me to the table, where he shoved me down onto my chair. He began to deal the cards, mine included.

The night dragged on and I was bored to death. Pim and Marmol grew tired of the game around midnight and decided to go to bed.

That night I went outside to run. When I came back around four in the morning, they were waiting for me in the caravan.

Marmol stood up and strode toward me, absolutely furious. He shoved me to the floor and told Pim to make sure I didn't move. Marmol went to get something out of a cupboard and came back with a leash. Pim watched him, perplexed. Marmol looked at me and said, "So you want to spend the night outside? Well, go right ahead."

He tied my hands behind my back, buckled the leash around my neck, and dragged me outside. I shouted at the top of my voice and struggled with all my strength. Marmol tied me to the caravan's tow bar and abandoned me there.

I cursed them, Marmol and Pim, as I fell asleep on the ground. I woke up after an hour, crickets and gnats flitting around my numb body.

In the morning Pim brought me a bowl of water and a few crackers.

"Marmol," he said, "he doesn't like it when you stand up to him. And he hates being taken for an idiot. You shouldn't play games with him. He'll always be cleverer and stronger than you. You can tell me where you've hidden what you stole."

I didn't say anything and he shrugged, turned around, and went off to the fountain to get washed.

When Pim came back, before he stepped into the caravan, I began to bark, just to annoy him. He gave me a dark look and walked over.

"Shut up, you filthy animal," he roared, kicking at me.

"To hell with you!" I cried.

He picked up a pebble and flung it at my face. Blood streamed from my nostrils and I passed out.

I was all alone. The G.I. paid me a visit. He spoke to me softly, like he was talking to a baby. He told me not to be frightened. He told me what to do, said I wasn't to get on the wrong side of Marmol. He was, he said, a dangerous and unpredictable man. I'd have to learn how to protect myself. If I'd been stealing, I absolutely had to give back anything I'd taken right away. I also had to find a way to escape. "But how?" I heard myself say. There was no reply, because just then something woke me up, there was something in my hair. I opened my eyes. The sky above me was unbearably bright. My head was ringing. A bird had landed on my head and got caught in my hair. The bird was cawing and struggling to get loose. It freed itself after a time and took off into the sky.

55.

It got cold and colder, and the rain continued unabated. Marmol released me after a week, and I went back to my bed in the caravan.

56.

Even though I cry a lot, I'm not an unhappy child. Truth be told, I'm cheerful, full of beans. I like being around other people, I'm not a child of the boys' home. I'm no orphan. I'm no dunce. I'm not a hoodlum. I'm a divine child. I'm an inner child. I'm a trickster.

57.

One afternoon I went into Sylvie's caravan without knocking. She lay naked on her unmade bed, lips parted, eyes sparkling, legs spread. Her pubis was hairless. Her heavy breasts heaved with difficulty, and her right hand played with a lock of hair that she brought coquettishly to her mouth. She beckoned me closer with a lazy wave of her hand, and she smiled. I closed the door and walked shyly over to her. She told me to get undressed and, as though hypnotized, I took off all my clothes without a thought. Standing naked beside the bed, I shivered with cold. She held out her arm and took my hand, pulling me closer. I lay down on her enormous fatty body. "I'll warm you up," she said, hugging me.

Stretched out across her body like a baby on its mother, snuggled up against her belly, my head between her huge breasts, I felt as though I was sinking inside her. Her flesh was soft as moss, her sweat mixed with mine, and I sobbed with pleasure. She stroked my hair, told me that she loved me, that she'd watch over me.

Suddenly a sensation I'd never felt before, a sensation I didn't know what to do with, took hold of my body, but Sylvie showed me how, and I discovered the warm moistness inside her. Five minutes later, drenched in sweat after a back-and-forth that she controlled with an expert hand, I fell back on top of her, like an overripe fruit onto a meadow, and fell fast asleep. I don't think she dared move and, when I awoke, she was still there beneath me, her enormous body protecting me, my shell. She smiled and motioned for me to leave. I stood up and got dressed, and went outside without a sound.

The next day she told me to come back and see her, which I did, and I spent another afternoon atop her fat belly.

58.

The woman with no limbs told me, "Careful now. Sylvie's a whore. She eats kids like you for breakfast."

59.

One time Marmol and Pim came back around five o'clock in the morning, three sheets to the wind. I heard them pissing behind the caravan. Marmol was hurling abuse at imaginary passersby, and Pim was giggling like a child. On his way into the caravan, Pim, out of sheer cruelty, strode over to my bed, grabbed me by the hair, and threw me to the floor. He accused me of making him mess up his routine the previous day, of not having ironed his shirt properly, of stealing a bundle of bank-notes he'd hidden under the sink. His eyes were angry and bulging like an animal's; saliva foamed at the corner of his mouth and he was streaming with sweat. He shoved me outside and punched me with his right fist. I fell to the muddy ground in a daze. Marmol came up behind Pim. Blind drunk and brandishing a cane, he beat me savagely as he roared with rage. I'd seen that cane before. It belonged to Ducal.

60.

Sylvie had trouble walking. She had trouble breathing, too, and would sometimes faint as she performed her striptease at the House of Horrors. "I'm so hot," she said. "I'm always too hot."

Sylvie went to see the doctor in Épinal. She asked me to go with her. She was wearing a feathered hat and a dress from another age. The sky was cloudy and it began to rain. She opened her big umbrella and took my hand. We strolled through the streets of Épinal and arrived thirty minutes early. I picked up a *Tintin* comic from a table in the waiting room. Soon it was Sylvie's turn. She managed to heave herself out of her chair. The other people waiting stared at her in disgust. She paid no heed to anyone as she walked to the doctor's office and stepped inside. I felt very alone without her. I no longer felt much like reading, I didn't feel much like doing anything. I waited there with my hands in my lap, breathing gently, my head empty.

Twenty minutes later, Sylvie emerged somberly, a huge worry line between her eyebrows. She collapsed onto a chair and began to cry. I stood up and walked over to her. I sat down beside her and laid my head on her shoulder. She rested her forehead against mine and her tears fell onto my cheeks. Suddenly she pulled away from me, got up, and headed for the door. I followed. It had stopped raining. The sky was white, the light harsh and unforgiving. Sylvie took my hand and said, "I thought it was up to me, but it's not..." I gave her a sidelong glance, not understanding. "I'm very ill," she said. "I'm going to die."

61.

Three days later, I went to see Sylvie in her caravan. I was just about to knock when I heard voices and sobbing. I walked around to the back of the caravan and found a half-open window. From there I could overhear the conversation. "I'm going to die. You must be happy. You'll be rid of me," said Sylvie, with a sniffle. A man's voice: "Don't be so melodramatic. You'll be better soon enough." It was Marmol's voice. "I'm not exaggerating," said Sylvie. "The doc says I don't have long to live. He got the test results back." Marmol began to laugh. "But you're a force of nature!" I heard Sylvie throw herself onto the bed and sob hopelessly. I looked in the window. Marmol went over to the bed and sat next to Sylvie. She couldn't stop hiccupping. Marmol touched her lightly on the shoulder. "Stop that," he said. "I don't like it when you cry." He stood up and began to walk away, but she called out, "Maurice, don't leave me!"

Maurice... I hadn't even known his first name. I knew it wasn't Cannabas, of course, but what a surprise to hear such an everyday name. Maurice! Maurice Marmol...

Sylvie propped herself up on an elbow and begged Marmol to stay. He turned, went back over to the bed, and lay down next to the teary-eyed fat woman. He stroked her hair. "Don't worry," he said, holding her tight. "Don't be frightened. Everything's going to be all right."

62.

Two months later, Sylvie was dead. I went to see her body at the morgue and felt very alone in the cold room. I'd been to plenty of wakes in the past, always with Max. Where was he now? My life in Mayerville seemed so very far away. Sylvie's belly had swollen during the night. She seemed to have doubled in volume. The odour in the room was burlesque, a blend of incense, patchouli, and death.

63.

Besides Marmol, Pim, and myself, no one came to the funeral. I was surprised to see that no one else from the troupe had bothered. "She wasn't very popular, you know," Pim said, sourly. It was raining. The gravedigger barely finished in time for the funeral. The earth was soft and hard to work with, and the hole needed to be bigger than usual, given her size. The poor man was exhausted, wheezing like a work-worn animal. I'd asked Marmol for some money to buy a bouquet of flowers, but he refused, so I ended up picking some tulips from a nearby garden. I put together a lovely arrangement and, before the gravedigger filled the grave with wet, barren earth, I tossed the flowers down onto the casket.

64.

I had a dream. There was a wall, a tall, red-brick wall with barbed wire on top. People came to admire it because it was so big. They also wondered why. What was the point? Why build a wall that reached almost all the way up to the clouds? And how could anyone get to the other side? Why build a wall without a door?

Suddenly I saw a young boy try to scale the wall. He was wearing crampons, but he didn't get very far. He fell back down onto the grass. He tried again, this time with slightly more success. He managed to climb a few metres, but then he slipped and toppled backward, shouting, "Dad! Dad!" His father, who had been looking everywhere for him, scooped him up. His mother came running over, crying. "Why did you run off?" she shouted. "Why did you run off?"

65.

Our next tour lasted six months. The magician drank more with every passing day. Business wasn't going well. Most of his acts had become badly dated. His performances had lost their charm. His hand trembled, his once-round belly was wasting away, his skin was yellow, his eyes wet with tears. Pim walked out on us. He disappeared overnight. Rumour had it he'd been arrested for breaking into a shop. Marmol started using me in more and more of his routines. I became his official assistant, for lack of a better option. For days at a time, I would practice coin tricks, palm cards, link Chinese rings, and work on my cup and ball routine. Even though Marmol could sense that travelling magicians would soon be a thing of the past, he went for one last hurrah, coming up with new illusions to replace the ones he'd been rehashing for years. He honed an impressive routine that involved me, after a series of complicated contortions, squeezing myself into a tiny transparent box. With great ceremony, the magician would cover the box with a sheet of black silk, sweeping it away to reveal, with a well-practiced smile, a little red fox that had taken my place, barking away for all it was worth and running frantically in circles. Then he would cover the box again, and with a wave of his magic wand I would reappear, in exactly the same position as before.

66.

Sylvie would come to me, stark naked, in my dreams. Her skin glistening with sweat, bags under her dark eyes, a broad nose, heavy jowls, tangled hair. She reeked of patchouli as she stood there in the moonlight in the woods. She was surrounded by forest animals. She would smile, beckon me closer. "I miss you so much," she'd say.

I dreamed of the day we went to the doctor. I would picture her that day, after her appointment, a mask covering her face. She'd sit down, hold her head in her hands, and when she took off the mask it would be Marmol's face I saw, and I would wake up screaming.

67.

I would spend all day and much of the night practicing magic tricks. My hands were constantly busy as I palmed cards and conjured coins. I practiced again and again. I didn't have the hands of a murderer. I had the hands of a magician.

68.

Marmol was losing a small fortune. Carnivals were increasingly given over to amusement rides, and the circuses and various attractions that accompanied them gradually began to disappear.

69.

One day, while I swept the floor of our little stage in the
big top, someone told me that the magician had fallen
into a river and drowned. Too drunk to swim. The next
day the woman with no limbs told me it was time for me
to go. I was free.

70.

Since we weren't far from the Vosges, I decided to walk
until I reached the forest. I walked for days, for nights
at a time. One morning I crossed a bridge over a river,
where a handful of boats and ducks bobbed, and arrived
at a clearing. There was an abandoned garden. The grass
was long, the flowers were wild; what had once been
pathways were now overgrown with moss. The trees
were unpruned and, in the middle of it all, there stood
a little shack with junk piled up all around it: a rusted
plough, a broken unicycle, an overturned wheelbarrow,
a rocking horse black with mould, the tyres from a
motorcar, a moped missing its wheels, a saw, a barrel
or two, an ancient push mower, and a thousand other
broken things.

A sign on the door read: "Healer."

I knocked.

The door opened and there stood a short man with
a round belly that pushed against his shirt, his eyes
glassy as though he'd been crying, his lips chapped,
and a pipe in his mouth, showing not the slightest surprise, as though he'd been expecting me. He told me to

come in and invited me to sit by the fire. He had been preparing his meal, a simple soup, and motioned for me to come share it with him. He offered me a glass of watered-down wine and a cigarette. The alcohol went straight to my head.

"Do you want me to heal you?" he asked, all of a sudden.

"Heal me from what?" I asked, more taken aback than curious.

"Well, I don't know. Any nausea? Colic?"

"My stomach is often sore... My teeth, too."

"Any other complaints?"

I didn't reply.

He came right up to me and tipped me back as if he were about to baptize me. He placed a hand on my forehead and said in a singsong voice, "I can cure you of all your ills."

I shivered. I suddenly felt very frightened of him.

After about five minutes, he let me go. He told me to stand by the fireplace and ordered me to empty my pockets. I laid out my playing cards, loaded dice, little scarves, elastic bands, and paper clips. He went off to get his remedies in the kitchen. When he came back, he rubbed my temples with a clove of garlic. Then he rubbed the glands on my neck with a yellow stone, sprinkled me with water that smelled of sulfur, and had me turn around three times. When he was done, he picked up the contents of my pockets and threw it all into the fire.

I stayed with the healer for a few days, perhaps a few weeks. I can no longer remember; I quickly lost all sense of time.

The medicine man didn't talk much. He smoked his pipe, fetched firewood from behind the house. I slept upstairs on a bed of straw in an alcove that wasn't quite a bedroom, a cubbyhole not big enough to stand up in. The healer slept in the kitchen, beside the door, as though afraid someone might come in during the night. I think he might even have kept a revolver under his pillow. "You'll heal, you'll heal," he kept saying over and over, and he made me all sorts of teas, mysterious concoctions that tasted of bergamot, buttercups, deadly nightshade, and snapdragon.

71.

"My child, there is no happiness without courage, nor virtue without struggle," the healer told me one evening, in a weary voice.

72.

I planted vegetables and harvested them when they were ready. I cooked from time to time. Occasionally I would get it wrong. The food would be too salty, too sweet, or not enough. I made little raffia baskets: red, green, and yellow. They soon filled the shelves and I thought perhaps I should sell them, but where?

73.

Despite the peaceful days and quiet nights, sometimes I would indulge in a fit of rage as my former gift for languages suddenly returned. I would let rip with a stream of insults directed at my mother, my father, my sister, and my brother. In those moments I hated the whole world, screaming and crying like a newborn baby terrorized at finding itself alive, then I would flop face down onto the pillow, hoping I'd suffocate.

74.

One day the healer, whose name I still did not know, said, "It's time for you to leave. You're healed."

I didn't say a word. He handed me a bag containing food and a few clothes. As I prepared to go, he grabbed my wrists and said:

"Look at your hands. They've stopped shaking."

"I hadn't ever noticed they shook."

"You were afraid, but now you're healed."

And with that he pushed me outside and closed the door behind me. I went down to the water and crossed the bridge, just like the day I had arrived. On the other side of the bridge, I stopped and turned to look back at the house. From a distance, it seemed to be floating in midair.

75.

Time passed.

Mating season returned, and I sat beside ponds and listened in delight to the croaking of infatuated frogs.

I stumbled upon a cave and settled down for the night.

One day when I was napping in the shade of a cherry-plum tree, I was awoken by whispering voices. I opened my eyes. Two men in uniform were standing over me. They had come for me. I put up no resistance, and they brought me back to the boys' home, where, waiting for me on the front steps, were the warden, the teachers, the supervisors, and, just in front of them, a little boy with a nose as pointy as a weasel's and dark, bluish circles around his eyes.

76.

They trimmed my nails and cut my hair, they scrubbed my body with coarse soap. The other boys were forbidden from asking me about my long abscondence. They admired my courage from afar and much was said about me, but I was left alone and quickly settled back into my old ways.

They had kept all my belongings, much to my surprise. They gave me back the blanket that Marie had knitted for me (a white label stitched into one of the corners spelled out my name in red thread: Émile), my Sunday best (which I had since grown out of), my game of jacks, a bag of marbles.

The little boy I'd seen the day I came back was the "editor" of the home's new monthly journal, which was full of drawings, short stories, fairy tales, and other children's writing. Ézéquiel—that was the editor's name—insisted on meeting me and immediately suggested I join his little team. I helped out with printing and I got the old press running again.

"Ézéquiel," I said. "That's an odd name."

He shrugged and said:

"That's what I'm called. I quite like it, as names go."

He asked me to write one or two articles to accompany some photographs he'd taken himself. I had a go and, amazed though I was to see my name appear in print, I didn't find my contributions especially successful, so I stopped.

I was born to work with my hands. I did the gardening. I learned how to tend to the fruit trees. I repaired broken doorknobs, chairs, and beds.

One day a posh couple came to see Ézéquiel. They were looking for a boy to adopt. Ézéquiel was asked afterward what he had thought of them. He said that didn't matter. All he wanted was the chance to leave the boys' home and start a new life, a life in which someone would buy him books, send him to school and university.

He left the boys' home one December evening. The posh couple loved him. They had come for him. It was raining and they sheltered Ézéquiel under a massive umbrella on the way out to their motorcar. I stood on the bottom step in front of the home. I waved a little as the car drove off, but Ézéquiel didn't look back.

77.

Surviving—not getting overly attached to people, not planning for the future, not dwelling unnecessarily on the past, keeping an eye on your things so they're not swiped from under your nose, never telling the truth, digging your fingernails into the palm of your hand or biting your tongue every time you want to cry.

78.

Living—the opposite of surviving. Being yourself, whispering "Fuck you" under your breath.

79.

The smell of the chestnut trees.
Conkers.
Chestnut purée.
Candied chestnuts.
Condensed milk.
Mi-cho-ko caramel candies.
The smell of glue.
The smell of paint.
Coloured stickers.
Iron-on transfers.
Unfinished football-sticker albums.
Party bags.

80.

Little Marie, I dream that you're my wife. I see you drunk, drunk with love, drunk with love for me. You walk through the village streets, happy, not a care in the world, beneath the August sun. It's summer, summer 1965. You're so happy to be alive, and you're on your way to meet me.

81.

My nights are restless. I dream nonstop, one nightmare slipping into the next. They stay with me for the rest of the day; I mull over every detail. One night I dream that Ducal—or perhaps it's the magician, their faces blur into one—comes to visit me at the boys' home. He finds me in my bed, runs a hand across my cheek and through my hair. Tenderly, he whispers in my ear, "Sleep, little boy. Sweet dreams." Then he takes down a guitar hanging on the wall and begins to play a lullaby. But he begins to strum louder and louder, and I'm suddenly very afraid that he'll wake the whole house. I try to speak up. But every time I go to say something, he puts a hand over my mouth. "Hush, hush. Be quiet, little one." All I want to do is leave, to get out of that bedroom where I shouldn't even be, to go back home. "Quit squirming," Ducal says. "Listen to the song I'm playing for you, just for you. And please be quiet. You're always talking, always looking for attention." Ducal stuffs his fingers in my mouth, then squeezes his whole fist in until I can no longer breathe. I beg him to stop, my eyes bulging. By the time Ducal removes his fingers from my mouth, they're covered in blood.

82.

Who will love me? Who would want me? I'll probably never marry. "You're as ugly as sin," my mother had told me one day, in a fit of anger.

83.

Another dream. Max and I break into Ducal's house again. He's gone to Paris for the week. We rifle through his things. I pass out. Max has gone. I hear moaning. He's being tortured. I sneak up. I peek through the keyhole and see Max lying across Cannabas Marmol's lap. The magician is whipping his bare backside. Max cries out in pain and shouts my name, Émile, for me to come rescue him.

84.

The days passed and nothing ever changed. I learned that my sister married a dentist. He was well-off. She was his secretary. My brother had left home and was now living alone in a one-bedroom flat on the outskirts of Nancy. He worked in a factory.

85.

I looked out the window. In the distance, a figure standing in the middle of the wheat field, a troubling silhouette that caught my attention, called out to me.

A scarecrow.

The scarecrow wore a large straw hat and a smock.

The scarecrow danced in the wind, its wooden legs bare beneath the smock, arms outstretched, waiting for summer to end.

86

A lady came to see me. She was my guardian, she told me. From now on I'd be living with her.

PART IV

Your heart's desire is to be told some mystery.
The mystery is that there is no mystery.

Cormac McCarthy, *Blood Meridian*

1.

Mireille Lemaire was a very sweet woman; she took me into her home in Grand, a small village of five hundred people notable for its ruins of a first-century Gallo-Roman amphitheatre.

I moved into a small bedroom that had been set up in the attic. A bed in the corner. A nightstand. A turquoise chenille blanket. A traditional wardrobe. A narrow window overlooking the garden. It was the first time I'd had a room to myself since leaving Mayerville.

2.

The first few days I got up at dawn and waited patiently at the kitchen table for everyone to come downstairs. Then, one Monday, I stayed in bed until eleven o'clock. Madame Lemaire came to see what was going on. I said, "I want to stay in bed. I don't feel well." She said, "My poor darling, I'll bring you breakfast." I turned my head to the wall. "No, thank you," I said wearily. "I don't want anything." She sighed as she went back downstairs.

I fell asleep and didn't wake until six o'clock that evening. Lying in the darkness, I thought of Max, little Marie, my brother, my sister, Jérôme, the healer, Marmol, Pim, Sylvie, Ézéquiel. I tried to recall their faces, but I couldn't.

Madame Lemaire came back up to see me just before supper. "You really should eat something."

She came over and sat on my bed. She put a hand to my forehead. "You don't have a fever. What's wrong? Does it hurt?"

I turned my head to the wall and said simply, "I'm tired."

3.

I'd stay in my room for hours. Because I liked being there, but mainly because I didn't dare go downstairs anymore. The Lemaires were kind and welcoming, and yet I didn't feel completely comfortable there. I tried not to grow too fond of Madame Lemaire, since I worried my stay would only be temporary and I would soon be placed with another family. Though my confidence grew with every month I spent in that cozy but ramshackle house.

4.

Madame Lemaire had four children: two girls and two boys. Lucie was a nuisance; I'm quite sure she hated me. Marianne was a quiet little girl, always clinging to her mother's apron strings. She was five, and still sucked her thumb. Jean-Luc was the same age as me—thirteen—but was much taller. Compared to him, I looked premature, sickly, a midget. Jean-Luc didn't say much, and didn't speak to me at all at the start, but little by little he began asking me questions, inviting me along for walks and lending me magazines. Olivier was eight, eyes wide and sparkling. He was scrawny, all skin and bones, and his head was too big for his body. Like a two-year-old child who never tires of the same game, he would play with me for hours at a time: draughts, ludo, rummy, tiddlywinks. I'd say, "Another round?" and he'd say "Okay." When I played with other children in the village, he would stay home, sitting at the kitchen table or sprawled on the grass, doing the same puzzle over and over again. His brothers and sisters called him Penelope. Sometimes he'd lose bits of the puzzle in the grass and fly into a rage. His siblings would look on, worried, frightened by such anger. When I was home, he would follow me around like a little dog. I didn't mind; I liked him.

Mireille Lemaire's husband sold cheese. He would leave early in the morning and come back at nightfall. He was a jolly man. He was used to talking to people. His children were a little ashamed of him—he always spoke at the top of his voice—but I thought he was hilarious.

I helped out, I gardened, I chopped wood, I washed floors. No matter how kind and generous Madame Lemaire was, I often railed against the world. I would lose my temper, clawing at my face and punching my head. I did all kinds of stupid things to test the limits of Madame Lemaire's patience, but she never once raised her voice, instead simply chiding me and explaining "the ways of the world." I told myself that my mother was right: I was nothing but a good-for-nothing, a hoodlum, a thief, a liar, you name it; I didn't deserve so much kindness from a woman who wasn't even my mother. But Madame Lemaire was patient and never seemed to lose heart. Sometimes I would find myself itching to call her "Maman."

5.

School was a struggle. I wasn't gifted. I forgot everything. I was only good with my hands. I could disman-
tle a radio and put it back together without a second
thought. I understood how every piece of machinery
operated, and I repaired things around the house. That
suited Madame Lemaire and her husband just fine;
he was often away and didn't have time to look after
the house. Given my disastrous performance at school,
Madame Lemaire told me one day that I couldn't go on,
I would have to find work. Madame Lemaire's husband
knew a man. I was sent for an informal interview, but
it went very badly. The Lemaires were told that I was
insolent and hot-headed, that I couldn't be trusted, that
I had stolen office supplies during the interview, that my
pockets were full of them. Mireille Lemaire, standing
with her back to the light, her hands resting on a chair,
said, "Not to worry, we'll try something else," then she
smiled a melancholy smile.

6.

My mother came to see me one Sunday. I couldn't
believe it; I hadn't heard from her in months. The last
time she'd visited me at the boys' home, she'd barely said
a word, still furious at me running away, appalled at my
cheek, my bad behaviour.

Madame Lemaire showed us into the dining room. It
smelled of mould. The staid tapestries on the wall, the
black stove, the cobwebbed logs stacked in a corner—it
all helped lend a feeling of hopelessness to a room that
was seldom used because it was so damp. My mother
sat in front of the big dresser where the preserves from
past seasons were stored on cool, dark shelves. Beneath
the table, our knees practically touched. She asked
me all about my new life. She shared the gossip from
Mayerville. I listened distractedly. She was surprised
that I didn't inquire about my father, brother, or sister.
She lit a cigarette. I wanted to tell her that Madame
Lemaire didn't allow smoking inside the house, but
I held my tongue. The smell of tobacco mixed with the
scent of her old bergamot perfume. She dabbed at her
forehead with a yellowed handkerchief that bore the

initials "LD." She spoke for a long time, gesticulating dramatically, tapping her ashes into a ceramic dish that was lying on the table, laughing at her own jokes. I was only half listening. I gazed at the little wrinkles around her eyes and mouth, I studied the lipstick she'd carelessly applied to her chapped lips, I observed her furrowed brow and the line that ran between her eyes. She wore her dull hair in a bun and loose strands escaped as she spoke.

Some time around four o'clock that afternoon, Mireille Lemaire brought in coffee and biscuits, wearing a broad smile. My mother sipped at her coffee, pulling a face. She watched me drop four sugar cubes into my milky coffee and asked me why. She said she didn't know where I got my sweet tooth from, no one else in the family had one. She began to talk about their money troubles. My father's business wasn't doing well. He was likely going to have to sell the bakery. She told me my father had been diagnosed with Parkinson's disease several months previously. She took me by the hand just before she left. I wanted to pull it away, but I let her. She sighed almost imperceptibly and sniffled, and her clammy little hand began to tremble in mine.

7.

Anthony Bloch owned a small electricity company just outside Nancy. He was looking for apprentices. Madame Lemaire's husband had known him for years; they had gone to school together, I think. Monsieur Bloch agreed to take me on without so much as meeting me. On my first day I was terrified that I would make a poor first impression, that he would say, "This young man is a cunning little fox, a good-for-nothing, a thief." But the first time Monsieur Bloch laid eyes on me, he looked at me like a shepherd looks at a sheep and put me to work at once. He taught me everything he knew, and very soon I had a real interest in the trade. I'd spend hours in the workshop, I'd go on jobs with him, I'd wield pliers and clamps, I'd thread copper wires through walls, I'd carry out repairs, I'd install heating systems and electric ovens, I suffered so many electric shocks that my hands became calloused and bruised. I'd come home at night exhausted but happy; for the first time in my life, I was earning a living, proud of my newfound skills.

Monsieur Bloch took me to a restaurant once a month. His wife would wear her fur coat and Eau de

Guerlain perfume. In summer, we'd go once or twice to Vittel, where we'd picnic by the water and swim when it was warm enough.

In the summer of 1960, the Blochs took me to see the sea. We visited Brittany and Normandy: a week of driving, roadside restaurants, and two-star hotels.

We also went to Alsace. Monsieur Bloch showed me the village where he was born. He told me about his family. His sister and father had died in Germany. His mother and brother had survived the concentration camps. His mother had come home pregnant. Bloch had been born premature, and almost died a few weeks later. He and his wife had no children. "Not after what my family went through," he told me when I asked if he had a son or daughter.

The Blochs had me over for supper. I didn't always know what we were eating, but it was delicious. Madame Bloch made lots of desserts, and I didn't hold back, having never been allowed them growing up.

Bloch's company grew and began to make a name for itself across Nancy; Bloch earned enough money to take on other apprentices. I trained the new ones. Monsieur Bloch said he was proud of me. He patted me on the back and laughed, his eyes crinkling.

8.

Little Émile, you're not scared any longer. Now you know how to use your hands. You were afraid you had the hands of a murderer, but the only thing they grasp are electric wires; you can rest easy, they'll never wrap themselves around the necks of little old ladies. You're a boy who has had his fair share of trouble, but you're no monster. You'll earn a living, get married, and have a son you'll care for and not send off to a boys' home. That is your wish.

9.

You shout your name over and over. You shout it until you're hoarse: Émile Claudel, Émile Claudel, Émile Claudel, Émile Claudel, Émile Claudel, Émile Claudel, Émile Claudel, Émile Claudel, Émile Claudel, Émile Claudel, Émile Claudel, Émile Claudel.

10.

Once I turned sixteen, I got a moped. I'd spend hours
on the road, going from village to village. I met loads
of other teenagers who were looking to have fun, move
and groove, drink, live their lives. It was the 1960s,
the decade of beat music and counterculture. Dancing
was everywhere; music was all around. Brigitte Bardot
was world-famous, a star. Paris was the fashion capital.
France had embraced modernity. I began going out to
bars, dances, discotheques.

I met a girl, Louise. I thought she was beautiful, I followed her everywhere. She let me kiss her, even feel her
up. She'd say, "You and your little suits, that cigarette in
the corner of your mouth, your slicked-back hair. You're
cute." But then one day I stopped hearing from Louise.
Someone told me she was getting married.

One night at a discotheque, I bumped into Laurice,
the girl from Mayerville who had wanted to show me
the ways of love. She was with a friend. They were sip-
ping cocktails and smoking Craven As. I went over to
them. Laurice recognized me and burst out laughing.
I sat down next to her. She told me she'd left Mayerville

and was living in Nancy, where she worked as a cashier. I paid for a few rounds and we had a nice time, laughing and poking fun at each other. Emboldened by the alcohol, I pressed up against Laurice, I was attracted to her. Her friend got up and went off to dance. I put my hand on Laurice's thigh and tried to kiss her, but she pulled away, a disgusted look on her face. She was as drunk as I was, but she'd stopped laughing. She moved over to the other bench seat. "What is it?" I asked. "What's wrong?" She just shrugged. "Don't you like me?" She sighed theatrically, stubbed out her cigarette in the ashtray, downed the rest of her drink, stood up, and made a dash for the exit. I never saw her again.

I would wander the streets of Nancy. I'd lurk around Rue de l'Épée and then, one night, I turned down it, holding my breath. I'd heard that was where the prostitutes turned their tricks. I tried to walk quickly, but it was like I was paralyzed, I could barely put one foot in front of the other. All around me, it was like a film was playing in slow motion. There were prostitutes by the dozen on that notorious street. I turned bright red. The women, not all of whom I found attractive, looked me up and down, called out to me, beckoned to me. When I got to the end of the street, not knowing what else to do, I lit a cigarette. I considered going back up the street, but suddenly I felt tired and ashamed. I turned left and walked away, quickening my step.

I came back the following day and went upstairs with the first woman I saw to my right as I turned down the street: a short, shabbily dressed blonde with chewed lips and bitten-down fingernails. She said her name was Chantal. I said that was my sister's name. She winced. She led me to a squalid bedroom, where air was in short supply and the walls were stained with shit or blood, it was hard to tell which. Chantal got undressed. She had scratches on her thighs, red marks on her arms. Regretting it right away, I asked without thinking, "You're not sick, are you?" and she shrugged and mumbled something incomprehensible. It was over in minutes. I was frustrated. I couldn't snuggle up next to that dry, bony woman, when all I wanted to do was, as I'd done with Sylvie, nestle up against a mountain of fat. There were no cozy folds, no ticklish rolls of flesh to be found on that woman. I stood, got dressed as fast as I could, left a banknote on the nightstand, and went out, slamming the door behind me. The corridor stank of sperm, piss, herring, and pickled vegetables.

Soon after, the very next day, I think it was, I went back to Rue de l'Épée. I had it all planned out. I'd walk past Chantal without so much as a glance. I didn't want to sleep with her again and, besides, I was more interested in the second woman a little further along the street, an older, rounder woman I'd noticed the first time. I turned down the street and saw, much to my relief, that Chantal wasn't there. I went straight up to the lady of my choosing. She spoke to me as though she'd known me forever, joked with me, chatted away. She said her name was Antoinette. I found her a little too affable; it felt forced. Once she undressed in the bedroom, I found her very bland indeed. I took an instant dislike to her. And yet, once in her bed, I closed my eyes and imagined I was touching Sylvie's skin, and I came as soon as I pushed inside her.

The following day I made a beeline for Catherine, a gorgeous woman I hadn't noticed the first two times. She was blonde, tall, and had a sophisticated look about her as she smoked. We made love like a long-time couple in her attic room. I became a regular. I liked her. Her body was soft and smooth; her movements, tender and considerate. Her bedroom window was always wide open. It was summer. The birds on the electric wires called cheerfully to each other and exchanged funny stories.

11.

At first, I didn't dare, and then one day I took the moped and rode all the way to Mayerville. It was still summer. My heart beat fast. I passed by the Bartroz house without stopping, but slowed down enough to be noticed. Marie was sitting on the green bench in front of the kitchen window. She was chatting with some kids from the village. She saw me and frowned. I thought she was going to call out to me, but no, she changed her mind. I went to the Potelon, but I didn't stop at my parents' place. I rode back down and passed by the Bartroz house again. Marie was still sitting outside, this time with her mother. The children from the village had disappeared. I slowed to a crawl, and when she saw me coming Madame Bartroz stood and put a hand to her chest. "My God! Émile, is that you?" she said. I stopped. "Hello, Madame Bartroz." Marie stood up, too. She said, "It *is* you. I thought I recognized you." I parked my moped in front of the barn. Madame Bartroz came over to me and took me in her arms, Marie pecked me on the cheek and blushed. Then Max came out of the house and walked over to me. I found him extraordinarily handsome. His skin was brown; the sun had burned it. He had a Gauloise dangling from his lips. "Émile?" He took a step back, looked at me suspiciously, and said, "It really *is* you!" I proffered a hand, but he took me in his arms instead and hugged me tight.

12.

"Did you know I was born with my eyes open?"

I didn't know what to say, so I replied:

"Really?"

"Yes," she said. "And do you know what that means?"

"No."

"That I see things how they really are."

It was a Wednesday afternoon. The sun was high. Marie and I were walking along Chemin de la Chavée behind the village. I was sweating in my leather jacket. She was wearing a gingham dress with a wide black belt, and a pair of flat shoes. She talked nineteen to the dozen. Mostly about her parents. Her home was a prison, she said. She couldn't dress as she pleased. Her skirts were always too short, her necklines too revealing, her heels too high. She couldn't wear the makeup she wanted. Her kohl was too pronounced; her lipstick, too provocative; the lines around her mouth, too vulgar. Her mother never let her out of her sight. She didn't like her spending time with boys. She'd once called her a harlot in front of the whole family just for chatting to three boys she didn't know late into the night and coming home with grass stains on her clothes. Madame Bartroz had spies everywhere in the village and beyond, Marie told me. People kept her mother informed of all her comings and goings, of who she was going out with, of how she walked down the street. Did she wiggle her hips? Did she strut about with one hand on her waist? Things were even worse in Paris: she wasn't allowed to go out, she had to come home straight after school. "I'm going to wind up an old spinster," she said with disgust.

I'd always thought of the Bartroz family as being very close and sophisticated, so I was surprised to hear Marie describing her parents as mean and conservative.

"They treat me like a little girl," she said, "I mean, I'm going to be fifteen soon."

Marie wanted to become a secretary. She was taking shorthand classes and learning to type. She planned to start earning a living just as soon as she could, so that she'd be independent. I asked her if she wanted to get married and have children. She just shrugged.

She told me she'd almost died once. Their apartment in Paris had no bathroom; they washed in the kitchen. The boiler hadn't been working and carbon monoxide had started to fill the apartment. She'd fainted and collapsed on the floor. Her mother had come home early from an appointment cancelled at the last minute to find her lying on the tiles. "Can you imagine?" Marie told me. "I nearly died."

I walked Marie home. Her mother had baked a plum pie. Madame Bartroz asked me if I wanted a slice.

I didn't dare say yes. "Go ahead, sit down," she said with a laugh. "Don't be so shy." She served me a slice on a little blue plate and made me a big bowl of coffee. "Would you like a slice, too, love?" she asked. Marie pulled a face and, without saying goodbye, went up to her room.

13.

Max and I saw each other regularly. At a discotheque one night, Max asked, "What do you think of my sister?" I blushed. He said, "You like her, don't you?" I laughed.

We asked a couple of girls to dance, then we sat back down and each lit a cigarette.

"You're too chicken," he said.

"Too chicken to do what?"

"To kiss my sister. He's too chicken, isn't he, Julien?" he asked, turning to his brother, who had just joined us.

"Oh yeah, way too chicken," Julien sneered.

"Kiss her and I'll give you fifty francs," said Max.

"Okay, fine," I laughed. "You'll see."

"Tomorrow, then. Kiss her tomorrow."

"Okay, tomorrow."

"Good! Don't chicken out now," he said, slapping me on the back.

14.

That morning was misty and humid. Marie and I had agreed to meet very early on Chemin de la Croix. "I absolutely have to see you," I'd told her. "Why so early?" she'd asked. "And why on Chemin de la Croix?" And I'd replied with a grin, "Do it for me, won't you? Don't ask questions." I parked my moped on the side of the road. I felt around in my pocket, took out an unopened pack of Gauloises, pulled a cigarette from it, and placed it carefully between my lips. I lit my cigarette, singeing my fingertips in the process, and spat out a few bits of tobacco that had stuck to my mouth. Marie was late. I waited patiently, still sitting on my moped, and lit a second cigarette.

I saw a silhouette approaching slowly in the distance. Marie was on her way. She was wearing her gingham dress with a greyish purple cardigan on top. She was shivering with cold. She came over to me. I kissed her on the corner of the mouth, almost on the lips. She recoiled a little.

We walked north along Chemin de la Croix. She chattered away, telling me all kinds of stories, but I wasn't really listening.

I asked her, "May I hold your hand?"

She didn't reply.

All of a sudden, she said.

"I know."

"You know what?"

"About the bet with my brothers."

"I've no idea what you're talking about," I stammered.

"Don't act all innocent, Émile. Your cheeks are bright red."

I flicked my cigarette butt into the field, where it landed next to a cow.

"It's fine," she said. "I want you to kiss me."

"You do?"

"Yes."

She stopped, closed her eyes, and opened her mouth ever so slightly. Waiting. I moved closer and took her by the shoulders.

First, I kissed her forehead, then her eyelids, which made her giggle, then I pressed my lips to hers and felt for her tongue. Her wet little tongue was soon curling itself around mine. I held Marie's body against mine. She smelled good: of Camay soap, Elnett hair lacquer, and Chanel No. 5. I tried to run my fingers through her hair, but it was too stiff with hairspray.

"Don't mess up my hair," she said, annoyed, pulling back a step. She gave me a sad smile.

I looked at her as if I were gazing upon a divinity, a sanctuary, an idol, a totem. She didn't move as she stared intently at me, her eyes burning, expressionless.

Suddenly a crow flew just over us, cawing as it swooped back and landed on Marie's head. I tried to shoo it away, and Marie writhed and thrashed, as though she had the Saint Vitus' Dance. It was a tame crow; I'd seen it before in the fields and around the village. It would land on windowsills, and people would feed it and pet it.

Marie was shouting and laughing at the same time.

Eventually the crow flew off.

We stood in the middle of the road for a long while, just looking at each other. I don't really remember what we said after that.

After a while, Marie turned and gave me a little wave before disappearing off into the morning mist.

I sat down on a rock and smoked a cigarette, the taste of Marie's sweet lips still all over my mouth.

15.

What are you thinking, Émile Claudel, you, the divine child, the inner child, the trickster, in this romantic moment, the mist-covered fields stretching out before you? And what is your sweetheart thinking, the young girl who has never known love, who has never been kissed by anyone but you? And what does the scarecrow you catch sight of in one of the fields want? It seems to be moving its lips, as though it's speaking to you.

16.

Max and I were on our way back from Tante Augustine's. Madame Bartroz had insisted that Max visit her. Tante Augustine was unwell. Max had asked me to go with him. We were treated to the usual stale biscuits that had an aftertaste of boiled cabbage as well as barley water that tasted like vinegar. The old woman regaled us with all kinds of stories, of which we understood not a word. She offered to answer any questions I might have about my father, but I said, "No, thank you. It's fine. I'm not really interested anymore." Max lit a cigarette as we left and handed me one along with his lighter.

We walked down the deserted backroad and didn't speak for a while. Then I said:

"Hey, guess what, you owe me fifty francs!"

"What?"

"You heard me. You owe me fifty francs."

The cigarette dropped from his lips and he slapped me on the back.

"Jesus! You kissed her? You? You kissed my sister?"

He bent down to pick up his Gauloise. He blew on it and wedged it back between his lips.

"Yeah, I kissed your sister. How about that?"

"I don't believe it!"

"Her lips are sweet and she smells good. I think I'll marry her one day."

He burst out laughing, then rummaged in his pockets and said:

"Hmm. I'll give it to you later. I don't have any money on me right now."

I looked at him, amused. We arrived back at his house. I hopped on my moped and left for Grand.

17.

The Bartroz family often invited me to stay for supper. Little Marie didn't always give me her full attention, flicking through magazines or listening to the
radio instead. Madame Bartroz took good care of me.
Monsieur Bartroz spoke to me about politics, current
affairs, the Communist Party, his time serving in North
Africa. Max and Julien joked around with me, treated
me like a brother. Marie couldn't sit still. She often
skipped dessert or coffee, eager to go outside and sit
on the bench by the kitchen window. Sometimes she'd
disappear off down the street and not come back until
late afternoon. I would still be there. Max, Julien, and
I would smoke on the green bench outside. The girls
from the village would walk by in a never-ending pro-
cession. Marie would come home wild-eyed, her hair
dishevelled. She'd say she was hungry, but when we sat
down for supper—"Émile, a bite to eat before you leave?"
Madame Bartroz would often ask—Marie wouldn't
touch a thing. She was watching her figure.

18.

One day my mother found out I'd been coming back to Mayerville without going to see her. She went to complain to Madame Lemaire, implying that I hadn't been raised right, which Madame Lemaire found at once insulting and ironic, refusing to invite her inside. When I came home from work, however, Madame Lemaire insisted I visit my parents. "I understand," she said. "But you must forgive them." I wanted to reply, "But how can a child forgive his parents when they abandoned him? How can they bear the thought of their child crying in the dark at night? How can they look him in the eye when they've done him so much harm?" But I held my tongue. I had too much respect for Madame Lemaire to go against her wishes, and I promised I'd see my mother and father the next time I went to Mayerville.

My parents invited me to stay with them for four days over the Easter holidays. I took them up on the invitation. My sister picked me up in the car. I was waiting for her in Madame Lemaire's kitchen, a small suitcase by my feet. Chantal had become a woman. She smoked menthols, had dyed her hair blonde, and was wearing a very chic grey suit. She smelled good, a new fashionable perfume. She gave me a big, dramatic hug. "He's so cute!" she said, ruffling my hair. She'd never liked me, had always made fun of me, but now she was behaving like a big sister who adored her little brother. She pinched my cheeks, clutched me tight against her, took my hands and shook them like she was possessed.

"Where have you been all these years?" I asked curtly as I got in the car. She looked at me in astonishment and started the engine without a word, but I spotted a tear glistening in the corner of her eye.

Before she parked the car in front of the barn, my sister said, "Try to be nice. They're glad you've come." My mother was in her kitchen, sitting in front of the fireplace, and my father stood by the window. They didn't move, so I stepped forward. I kissed my mother. Her eyes were wet; she clutched a little handkerchief in her hand. I went over to my father. He gave me a hug. A long hug. Too long, if you asked me. I would have preferred the whole scene to be less theatrical, less forced.

I asked how my brother Michel was doing. My parents didn't see much of him now that he lived in Tomblaine, a suburb of Nancy. For a long time, there had been no girlfriend in the picture, but he'd recently married a woman he'd met at the zoo in Nancy. She was much younger than him and came from a relatively poor family of twelve children, of which she was the youngest. Michel hadn't invited a soul to his wedding.

335

My mother had cooked a Sunday roast and her sticky beans. There was even dessert, which she served on her blue-and-white-striped Foxtrot plates. She'd made her trademark floating islands, which I'd seldom been allowed as a young child. I found them too sweet: the saccharose stung my palate and I wasn't able to finish my plate.

Lunch passed without incident, almost in silence, my father chewing loudly and dropping food on the napkin he'd tied around his neck. There was a pharmacopoeia of medicine bottles lined up beside his glass: tablets, syrups, drops. His hands shook. My mother barely ate. My sister, sitting just beside her, watched me out of the corner of her eye. She kept running a hand through her hair and fidgeted constantly. My mother turned a little in her direction and shot her a look, lips pursed. After a time, my sister lifted her head toward me and mumbled something I didn't make out. I asked her what she'd said, but my mother elbowed her and my sister said with a pained look, "It's nothing."

After dessert, I went for a walk around the garden and smoked a Gauloise. The gardener was raking the path. It was no longer Gérard Thiebaut, but a younger man. Gérard Thiebaut had been found dead in the woods. People said he'd been drunk and had fallen head first against a fountain. A half-empty bottle of wine was found beside him. There was a rumour circulating that he'd been murdered. Suspicion fell on Ducal, since the pair had been seen one week earlier, arguing by the side of the road. Ducal had been spotted raising his cane high

336

into the air as though about to thrash Gérard Thiebaut with it, but the gardener had stepped back just in time. Apparently, Ducal had shouted all kinds of things at him, and kept repeating my mother's name.

"Pleased to meet you," the new gardener said, shaking me by the hand. I found him very polite. The garden had seen better days. The rose bushes were straggly; the privets, bare; the trees, sickly. I sat down on a dusty deck chair beneath the arbour and smoked a cigarette. I blew smoke rings as I watched the gardener work. He'd taken off his undershirt, and I admired his muscular chest. He wore a gold chain with a medal of the Blessed Virgin around his neck. He reminded me of the Gypsy, who had left the village and never been seen again. Some said that he too was dead; murdered, according to certain people. Something about a revenge killing, but then again people used to say all kinds of things.

After half an hour, I went back into the house and up to my room. Nothing had changed. I went over to the window and looked across the street. Ducal's house was falling apart. Tall grass had overrun the front garden, building stones had fallen to the ground, the roof was in ruins. And yet Ducal still lived there. It was just that no one ever saw him. He was hiding, people said, because he'd become hideously ugly with age. "No change there then," I thought. He was treated like an old bully and no longer invited anywhere. People wondered what he ate, since they never saw him go out for groceries. He'd never had a vegetable garden, so he couldn't be feeding himself that way either.

I was daydreaming, standing there in front of the window, a Gauloise hanging from the corner of my mouth, when I heard my mother call up the stairs. "You left your suitcase in the hall," she shouted. I told her I'd be right down. "Don't bother, I'll bring it up," she said, irritated. "It's in the way. You left it right in the middle of the hall!" The ash dropped off the tip of my cigarette and down onto the floor. I heard my mother struggling with the suitcase as she made her way up the stairs, stopping on every warped step that creaked beneath her feet, sighing out of tiredness or perhaps anger. I threw my cigarette butt out the window and went to meet her. By the time I reached the landing, she was already on the top step. I held out my hand to take the case, but I must have moved my hand or else she did, I'm not sure, it was as though I'd pushed her or else she'd just let herself fall and she lost her balance, letting out the shrill cry of a rat being slaughtered and, without even having time to catch herself on the banister, she toppled backward. A first bump, then a second, then I heard her cry, "My leg!" and then silence. I put my hand to my mouth, the same feeling as when Max and I had set fire to the barn: guilty, horrified, but also terribly excited and doubtful all at once. A feeling that nothing was real, a curious ether between two mysterious worlds: on one side, everything was real; on the other, a parallel universe, a magical, monstrous world where everything was permitted.

19.

I stood there, motionless, for several minutes. I think I might even have sat down on the top step to smoke a Gauloise. Slowly, savouring every puff. Then, I walked down the stairs to my mother's body lying there on the tiles, one badly hurt leg folded over the other. She was unconscious, blood trickling from her temple.

20.

My mother was rushed to the hospital in Neufchâteau. She'd fractured her leg and hip. During her fall, her leg had struck an old iron bar that jutted out of the stairs and had never been straightened. An open wound ran from her knee to her ankle. My mother didn't want to see anyone, only my father. The wound continued to ooze pus in spite of the doctors' attentions, though my father was convinced everything would turn out for the best—until, that is, the day the doctor told him his wife's wound had become infected and was gangrenous.

I went back to Madame Lemaire's. She greeted the news with a sad smile. I didn't go to the hospital; my mother didn't want to see her children.

21.

Two weeks later, my sister showed up at Madame
Lemaire's. She knocked timidly on the door and came
inside. Her teeth were chattering. She seemed over-
whelmed with emotion. I was playing cards with Olivier
at the table. Chantal's eyes were glassy, she looked like
she'd come undone. Madame Lemaire asked her if she'd
like to sit. Chantal collapsed onto a chair and put her
head in her hands. She breathed heavily for a moment,
took her hands away from her face, spread them out flat
on the table, and, lifting her head a little, but without
looking us in the eye, staring off into space, she whispered, "They had to amputate her leg."

22.

Your heart's desire is to be told some mystery. The mystery is that there is no mystery.

23.

Back home after several weeks in hospital, my mother was still in the upstairs bedroom. We could have carried her downstairs in her chair, dangerous though the stairs were, but she didn't want to. The drapes were drawn all through the day. The window was never opened. It hurt my father to see my mother withdraw from the world and fall into a depression from which he feared she would never recover. He had trouble looking after her and the bakery. Michel moved back home for a spell and helped my father in the shop, then he left again. Chantal came to watch over our mother. She stayed in her old room. She took control of everything. She was the only one, it seemed, who could perk up our mother's spirits, and after a few weeks my mother began accepting visits from the neighbours.

I went to see my father at the bakery. I watched him go about his work, kneading the dough, preparing the brioches. He moved slowly. He'd lost his agility. He didn't talk much, he was a little awkward, but there was something fundamentally honest about him. He'd changed, I thought. Parts of his face reminded me of mine, the way he held his cheek while lost in thought was something I did, too, and we had the same big ears, the same droopy eyelids, the same hooked nose. There was no two ways about it: we looked like each other. Did that mean my father really was my father? Whenever we talked about it, Max would point out that there were still some loose ends—why did the dates not line up?—but what did it matter, in the end, I thought.

Not long after that, my father stopped working. His Parkinson's was getting worse. He walked ever more slowly, his hands trembled nonstop. Given his failing health, and with business not what it had once been, he was forced to sell the bakery.

24.

One day my mother asked to see me. I rode in from
Grand on my moped. I went into the kitchen and was
stunned to see Ducal sitting by the window, smoking
a cigarette. People had been calling him decrepit, but
I didn't see any change. Ducal stood and came over to
me with his hand outstretched. Perhaps he was going
to strike me, but I wasn't afraid. He took my right
hand and shook it. "How you've changed, little fox!"
I shrugged and pulled my hand away. "Your mother's
waiting," he said. "She's upstairs in her room. Don't
tire her out. She's fragile." I turned on my heel and,
before leaving the kitchen, I asked where my father
was, but Ducal was no longer there: he'd disappeared.
I went upstairs, turned right, walked through my
brother's room, and entered my parents' room. Lying
there on the bed, her arms on the eiderdown, stretched
out on either side of her body, my mother looked at me
tenderly.

She told me to sit on the edge of the bed and immediately began to sob. I patted her awkwardly on the shoulder.

"Don't cry, Maman. Don't cry."

I rested my head on her shoulder and, in a moment that didn't feel entirely real (might it have been a dream?), she ran her hand through my hair, slowly, and I heard her sob, and I too was crying. I pulled away and kneeled by her side. I rested my head on the eiderdown and fell asleep as she continued to stroke my hair.

Roused by my own snoring, my mouth dry, I resurfaced a half hour later. My mother was sleeping quietly, arms folded across her chest. Her long hair fell around her shoulders. She looked like she was dead. A fly had landed on her right eyelid. Her lips were purple. I got up slowly, without a sound, and tiptoed out of the room. But she suddenly shouted, "Émile!" and I went back. She was still asleep, but she seemed delirious. She babbled words I didn't understand, rhyming off names, including my own, but also my father's, and the G.I.'s, too. Jack, Jack Kingston.

25.

A few kilometres from Contrexéville was a small village of two hundred and fifty souls by the name of Ramonville. There was nothing special about it, but every weekend it attracted a crowd of young people from the surrounding area and as far away as Haute-Marne, Haute-Saône, Meuse, and Meurthe-et-Moselle. In days gone by, people used to come from all around on Saturday nights to dance to the music of accordionist Jean Lhuillier. The dance hall was enormous, and lovers would scratch their names on the walls in big, capital letters.

Now they came to jive, to twist, to dance the jerk. Marie, her brothers, and I would go there every Saturday. Marie would crimp her hair, apply a thick layer of eyeliner, and put on pale, almost white lipstick. I'd wear a skinny tie, pointy shoes, tight-fitting suits. My hair was short, with a cowlick at the front. A Gauloise dangling from my lips. Max really was good-looking: tanned face, frizzy hair, leather jacket with a fur collar. Julien would be wearing slim-fitting trousers, a gaudy short-sleeved shirt. He was younger than we were, but already going out. He went everywhere with us. And then there was Dédé, Riri, Alex, Ray, Dany, Isa, and all the others.

Marie and I would enter dance contests. We won a twist competition one summer. I went home with a fantastic lighter and Marie got an enormous bouquet of flowers. She kissed me on the cheek and said she'd never been so happy in all her life.

26.

One day I asked, "Where's Ducal? I haven't seen him around." My father replied, "He's dead! Didn't you know?"

27.

Little Marie had drunk too much. It brought out her mean streak. "I want to be free," she cried. "I don't want to get married." I looked at her with a pained expression and she stared back at me, her eyes glassy, as though she hated me.

28.

Little Marie, you dream of becoming an air hostess. You picture yourself up in the clouds on a Caravelle jet, and you smile.

29.

One day my father, a man of few words, told me, trembling all the while, "I've made such a mess of my life."

30.

It was Max's birthday. He'd invited all his friends. Everyone buzzed around him. I was so proud to be his friend.

Just before dessert, I saw Marie get up from the table. I stood up and followed her. She went to sit on the bench in front of the kitchen window by the road.

"What's wrong?"

"Nothing."

Silence. I wanted to take her by the hand, but she had her arms folded.

"Would you rather I left you alone?"

She shrugged.

"Go," she said. "Or stay, it's all the same to me."

I rummaged in my pocket for my pack of cigarettes, but I couldn't find it. I must have left it on the kitchen table. I went inside to get it and when I came back out Marie had disappeared.

31.

We were in a discotheque in Nancy. Marie, Max, Christelle (Max's girlfriend at the time), Julien, Dédé, Alex from Coussey, and Isabelle from Neufchâteau. The music was blaring; we could barely hear ourselves talk. The table was cluttered with glasses, bottles, cigarette packs, and overflowing ashtrays. "Do you like my dress?" Marie asked Dédé. "Yes," he said. "Of course. It's very pretty." She got the hiccups and began to glare at Isabelle, who was sitting on the other side of the table. "Not like Isabelle's dress," she said. "Where did you find it? In a bin somewhere?" She began to laugh, a loud, nasty laugh. The people at the neighbouring table turned around and smiled. Isabelle turned bright red. She stood and ran to the toilet. Max was embarrassed and gave his sister a dirty look. Julien said to Marie, "Why don't you go dance for a bit and stretch your legs?" Max said, "She won't be able to stay on her feet." "Oh, shut up and drink your beer," retorted Marie.

Isabelle came back after a while. The front of her dress was all wet. Marie burst out laughing and jumped to her feet. She tottered off to the toilet in turn. She came back a half hour later.

"Where were you?" asked Alex.

"I fell asleep on a chair."

"In the toilet?"

"Yeah, in the toilet."

"You're really something else," said Isabelle, blowing the smoke from her cigarette at Marie.

"What do you mean, something else?"

Isabelle shrugged.

Marie suddenly fell asleep and dozed for a few minutes, her head against the wall, her mouth wide open. Then she woke with a start and leapt up. "It's so hot in here!" she said. She reached into her dress and emerged with her brassiere, which she flung behind her. Then she removed her shoes and hopped off in the direction of the dance floor, clapping her hands as she went. She began to wiggle her hips and shake her hair. I followed after her, took her by the arm, and held her tight to calm her down. I could feel her little breasts against my chest. She rested her head against my shoulder and we danced a slow dance even though the music was much too fast.

Later that night, arm in arm, Marie and I walked out of the discotheque.

"Did everyone think I'd had too much to drink earlier?" she asked me. "Not at all," I replied. "You're sure?" she insisted. "It's kind of embarrassing." "Yeah, I'm sure," I said.

32.

With my pay, I bought myself a record player, LPs, and singles. I listened to *Pour moi la vie va commencer*, over and over again. My life was set to begin.

33.

One afternoon I spotted Marie in Neufchâteau. She was walking into a florist's with a boy I didn't know. He bought her a bunch of anemones. Marie snorted with laughter, her cheeks aflame. He leaned in toward her, as though about to kiss her, but she made a face and shook her head. They came out of the shop. He tried to take her arm, but she shrugged him off, visibly irritated, although they continued to walk side by side. I stood there, my hands in my pockets, a Gauloise in the corner of my mouth, and watched them walk off down the road.

34.

The following day, I presented Marie with a big bunch of roses. She let out a little shriek of surprise. Her mother was there, filled with wonder at such a fine bouquet; Monsieur Bartroz smiled. "They're lovely," Marie said shyly. I looked around, but I didn't see the anemones anywhere. Madame Bartroz went off to get a vase, and filled it with water. She cut the stems and put the roses in a crystal vase on the kitchen table. With every passing day, a few petals would drop onto the wax tablecloth. I counted them each time I visited. Soon the water in the vase began to smell, and one day I saw my sad bouquet of faded flowers on the neighbours' manure heap.

35.

Max, Julien, and I were partying through the night with a bunch of friends. We were at Dédé's. The music was turned up as loud as it would go. Julien was dressed up as a woman. I followed suit, putting on a miniskirt and high heels, outrageous makeup, and a blonde wig. Max laughed when he saw me. Then, once we were in the village, my friends ran off, or else I got lost, I'm no longer sure which. I took to the paths behind the houses. I spied on people through the windows of their cozy homes. Steaming drunk, I stood for the longest time before a large living-room window, watching three children playing with their Lego. They were building some sort of complicated boat. The parents were busy in the kitchen. The entire scene exuded happiness and love. There was no fear in that household; the lamps bathed the home in a warm glow.

One of the three children, a little boy, stood up and went over to the living-room window. He put his hands against the glass and moved his face closer to peer into the darkness. I took a step back, not wanting to be seen in my getup. My high heels were covered in mud, my

wig was askew, my makeup had run. But the little boy
had seen me. He lifted his hand and waved. I stepped
back again and took off along the tree-lined paths. As
I ran, my wig caught on a branch and it stuck there, a
decadent sight in the starry night.

36.

"I'm scared."

"Scared of what?"

"Everything."

Marie was wearing a white flowery dress. We were in a café in Neufchâteau. Cigarette smoke hung thick beneath the fluorescent lights. A Richard Anthony song played on the jukebox. The smell of roasted coffee, hops, Elnett hair lacquer, and Chanel No. 5.

"I'm scared to have sex."

"Why would you be scared?"

"Because," she said very quietly, "I'm afraid it might hurt."

I didn't know what to say, so I just stroked her forearm.

"And I'm scared of getting pregnant."

She pulled her arm away and massaged it gently as though I'd hurt her.

"I sometimes get scared, too, you know."

"You?"

"Yes. I'm scared of losing control of my emotions. I'm scared the rage inside me will all come flooding out."

Marie gave me a thoughtful look.

"I never talk about it, but the boys' home was a very difficult time for me."

"I don't understand," said Marie, "why your parents just got rid of you like that. My mother says that was irresponsible of them."

"She said that?"

"Yes. And it really hurt Max, you know, losing his friend like that."

"He might have come see me more often. I think he only visited me once."

"Once?" she asked. "Are you sure about that?"

I ordered another coffee from the waiter as he passed by.

"It wasn't easy for him," she went on, "seeing his best friend in that miserable place. He was afraid our parents would send him there, too. He'd started misbehaving at school, he'd become withdrawn. He and I weren't getting along at all. Sometimes he'd hit me. He didn't go with us to Mayerville for two years in a row. He stayed behind with an aunt in Paris."

I didn't say anything, so she went on.

"But now he's your best friend. It just goes to show: it all works out in the end."

"It's true, everything works out in the end," I said, finishing the rest of my coffee.

37.

I didn't see her at first. She was at the end of the street, a bag in her hand, sunglasses and a scarf on her head. She looked like a movie star, a younger, shyer Brigitte Bardot. I hid in a carriage entrance and watched her walk past, slowly, whistling a tune. I followed her, excited by her bum in her tight-fitting skirt. Small and dainty as a child, she made you want to protect her, hold her in your arms, make a fuss of her. She glanced at her watch, then began to walk faster. She forged straight ahead, paying no one the slightest heed, even jostling an old lady who, she must have thought, wasn't walking quickly enough. I followed Marie from street to street, crossing the road whenever she changed sides. Where was she going? Was she off to meet a lover?

As I walked behind her, I suddenly noticed the hair spilling out of her scarf. It was the colour of gold; she'd dyed her hair blonde. She stopped abruptly outside a bar and gave a little wave through the window to a young man sitting inside. He stood up when he saw her. She opened the door and went over to him. He kissed her on the mouth. I watched them from across the street.

She'd taken off her scarf and her blonde, almost white hair blazed in the light. The young man handed her a Marlboro and she took it. She didn't know how to smoke and held the cigarette in her fingertips, coughing out the smoke. I watched her lean forward a little and laugh as she choked. The stranger ordered her a glass of white wine and she drank it all in one go, then another that she drank just as quickly. They chatted and then, after a while, she jumped to her feet, as though they'd been arguing. She put her scarf and coat back on, picked up her bag, and left the bar without saying goodbye. She didn't look back when the man she'd been with followed her to the door and shouted, "Marie! Marie! Come back!"

If I'd been carrying a gun, I would have shot him, there and then, without warning. If I'd been carrying a knife, I would have stabbed the stranger with it, made him bleed. I started following Marie again. She walked quicker and quicker, she was in a panic, holding her scarf with her right hand as it threatened to blow off. The weather had turned. It was suddenly very windy; it was going to rain. I lost sight of her at a busy crossroads. I went into a bar and ordered a beer. Tears breaking at the corners of my eyes, I downed my glass and asked the barman for another.

38.

My life was set to begin.

39.

My mother stayed in bed for a long time. Once again, she refused to see anyone, until, that is, she grew tired of my sister, who was becoming ever more controlling. Chantal had sold some of the furniture and dismissed the gardener. She maintained we'd run out of money, even though she'd just had the whole living room redecorated. Rumour had it my mother had inherited money from Ducal, but I didn't believe a word of it. My mother was getting back into the swing of things. They'd given her an artificial leg; she was getting used to it. She did the gardening, dressed in a blue smock, and spent hours trimming the rose bushes, planting vegetables and flowers. She did it all alone, without stopping to rest. The work made her tired, which seemed to put her in a good mood. Although she'd never been much of a reader, she began reading novels by Guy des Cars and Gilbert Cesbron. Sometimes she would fall asleep in the afternoon heat, on a deck chair beneath the arbour. She looked almost comical with her moustache, her eyebrows that almost touched. Ever since she'd been left handicapped, she'd become more amiable, more patient.

She'd go for walks in the village. People would say hello to her, embarrassed.

One day I was on my way back from Max's when I found her sitting by the fountain across from our house, smoking a cigarette. The sun was in her eyes, and she didn't see me approach. She gave a start. She raised a hand to her forehead and squinted. She could make out a silhouette against the sunlight, but she still didn't recognize me. "Maman, it's me!" I said. "Oh, it's you, Émile," she said, all surprised. I asked, "What are you doing out here all by yourself?" She answered, "What does it look like? I'm smoking a cigarette." When I looked down, I could see a few letters poking out of the pocket of her housedress. Then I looked up and saw her eyes: they were wet. "Come on," she said, stubbing out her cigarette on her shoe. "I'm making jam. You can give me a hand." And she stood up.

40.

The dead no longer love the living. That's what they tell me. They come to me at night. The young boy who drowned in his bath came to speak to me. He explained that he'd wanted to die, but he was sorry he had. He really wanted to come back and ask his parents not to forget him. He could tell they'd grown used to life without him. All the old folks in the village that Max and I had been to see on their deathbeds, they visit me. They tell me their stories, they tell me about their lives, how they died. They tell me their secrets, why they're really dead. They say, the living loved us, but now they neglect us, they forget us, they don't love us like they used to, they sometimes say unkind things about us, so that's why we're taking our love back, to protect ourselves. That's why we the dead no longer love the living.

41.

I took Marie for a spin on my moped. We went to Grand. Madame Lemaire made us a meal. Marie and I went up to my room. She saw that I still had the little blanket she'd knitted me, that I kept it at the end of my bed. She saw, on the coat stand, the woolen scarf she'd given me one day before she left for Paris. "You still have those old things," she laughed. I was a little piqued, and replied, "They're not that old, Marie. We were still children just yesterday." She rolled her eyes, a little smile on her lips, then went to the window and her expression suddenly grew serious. I didn't like it when she looked sad like that. Her dark eyes were lost to the shadows. She was no longer with me. I spoke to her, called out to her, but she remained in that abyss, as though she didn't want to free herself from it.

I drove her back to Mayerville. Just before we reached the village, we stopped in a field and lay down beneath a plum tree.

"Show me your hands," she said.

"What? What's wrong with my hands?"

"They're absolutely massive. You have big, fat fingers."

"You think so?"

"Look," she said, taking my hands. "They stretch all the way around my neck. They're like a killer's hands."

"What?"

"You know, like in the movies. The killers always have big, flat hands, with scaly fingers. You have the hands of a killer."

I rolled across the grass and away from her. I took a crumpled pack of cigarettes from my pocket. I took out a Gauloise and lit it with the lighter I'd won at the twist contest and smoked in silence. Marie stayed where she was, just a few metres from me, not moving, facing the other way. "Fine," she sighed. "I'm leaving." Then, as she stood up, "My mother's expecting me. Bye!"

I watched her go: her gingham dress, her slender legs, her flat shoes now stained a little green. She was so beautiful.

42.

We didn't see each other for several weeks. Then, one day, as I was riding past her house, she was sitting there on the bench, wearing stiletto heels and a tight-fitting, flowery dress. She looked funny with her hair done up in a beehive. She gave me a little wave and told me to stop. I parked my moped.

"Come sit beside me, you big idiot," she said.

I got off my bike and sat beside her.

She took my hand in hers and said:

"You have lovely hands. I didn't mean what I said. I can be nasty sometimes. I don't mean to be."

We stayed there for a long time without speaking.

And then, resting her head on my shoulder, she said, "Let's get married."

43.

As I drove into the wind at top speed, I happened to pass by the boys' home. I stopped my moped. The wind picked up even more. I stayed there for a long time, my hands on the bars of the gate. I shivered. A shutter had come partly off its hinges and was now banging against the front of the building. I thought about the other boys. I pictured myself at the reunion in ten, twenty years' time, and I began to cry.

The leaves were blowing about in the wind. The clouds were low in the sky. It started raining. I got back on my moped and headed east.

44.

I could turn into a little animal with prickly red fur, pointy ears, a long snout, keeping its back low, dragging its whisky-coloured tail. I could also, on occasion, turn into a wolf, an owl, a doe, and disappear off into the forest. I have more than one means of escape, but I decide to stay right where I am, both feet planted firmly on the ground, like an unshakeable tree, half dead, but impossible to uproot.

45.

The Bartroz family went back to Paris. Max stayed in Mayerville with his grandmother. He'd found work not far from Neufchâteau and was going out with a girl from Liffol-le-Grand. Solange Lecuyer was delighted to be spending the winter with her beloved grandson. They looked alike: the same smooth skin, frizzy hair, dark eyes, snub nose. Max and I were seldom apart. I'd go over to see him at his grandmother's or he'd come to my host family. We'd go out every weekend. Marie would write me long letters from Paris. She was bored, she said. She'd draw three little red hearts beneath her signature. I would stare at them long and hard, as though they were a code to be deciphered.

46.

It was my birthday.

My mother had invited me over for supper. When I went into the kitchen, she was sitting on a straw chair, reading a book by Guy des Cars. She looked up and said, "I made boeuf bourguignon, floating islands, and a chocolate cake." She put her book down on the window ledge and stood up. I helped her set the table.

During the meal, my mother asked me all about my work, about my boss, Monsieur Bloch. "I must invite them over one day, him and his wife," she said. My father was quiet, his eyes subdued. His hands shook. "Why not?" I said, trying to sound enthusiastic. In the past, my mother couldn't abide people making conversation at the table, but now she wouldn't stop jabbering on. She told me all the latest village gossip. I only half listened, instead focusing on the wrinkles on her forehead, and on her thick makeup. When the time came for dessert, she handed me an envelope that contained a musical birthday card with a few banknotes inside. Before I left, she took my hands and squeezed them a little too hard. She kissed me, then collapsed down onto a chair, suddenly looking deflated. She rested her elbows on the table and propped up her chin with her hands, her lips twitching like an old woman's.

My father was staring off into the distance. I leaned in close and kissed him on the forehead. His left hand trembled on his knee.

I went outside and climbed onto my moped. It was getting dark. I started the engine.

Outside the tobacconist's, at the fork on the main street, I suddenly saw Max, a carton of cigarettes under one arm. He was rooted to the spot, staring blankly ahead. I stopped. He looked pale and, since he still hadn't said a word, I asked:

"What's the matter? You should see the look on your face!"

"You haven't heard?"

"No... heard what?"

"John F. Kennedy's been shot."

"What?"

"Someone just shot the president of the United States. In Dallas. JFK is dead."

I got down off the moped and we walked over to his house. I pushed the handlebar with one hand and puffed nervously on a Gauloise. When we reached Max's, I parked my moped beside the green bench.

We listened to the news on the kitchen radio. "Such a sorry business," said Solange Lecuyer as she came out of her bedroom, wearing her dressing gown and dragging her feet as she went. After the news, Max turned off the radio and the three of us sat around the table without saying a word.

After a little while, I stood up and said, "I'd better go. It's getting late." Max got up, too. He said, "Hang on, I got you a present, for your birthday." He went upstairs and came back down holding a Françoise Hardy record, *Le Premier bonheur du jour*. "Happy birthday!" "Thanks," I replied, blushing. "See you next week, I'm working this weekend," he said, walking me to the door.

I sat on the moped and started the engine. Max lit a Gitane and came over to me. He slapped me on the back with his left hand. His eyes were wet; his brow, furrowed. I gave him a smile and headed west, back toward Grand.

The wind beat hard against my face. My thoughts turned to Marie's sweet lips, and to the future; to John F. Kennedy's widow and poor little John-John, who no longer had a daddy.

It was November 22, 1963. I'd just turned eighteen.

Author's Note

This novel includes a number of uncredited references, including 'Twilight,' a poem by Charles Baudelaire, translated here by Cyril Scott; two Kurdish proverbs; and a line taken from *Emile, or On Education* by Jean-Jacques Rousseau.

Éric Mathieu is a professor at the Department of Linguistics at the University of Ottawa and a writer. He studied at University College London and has lived in Canada's capital since 2004. His first novel, *Les suicidés d'Eau-Claire* (La Mèche), was a finalist for the prestigious Trillium Book Award in 2017. *Le Goupil*, published in French by La Mèche and now translated as *The Little Fox of Mayerville*, is his second novel and the first to appear in English.

QC FICTION

Current & Upcoming Books

Visit **qcfiction.com** for details and to subscribe
to a full season of QC Fiction titles.

Printed by Imprimerie Gauvin
Gatineau, Québec